Love & Lust

Learning the True Meaning of Love

By Gerald C. Anderson, Sr.

ISBN: 978-1-957333-18-2

Lyfe Publishing

Publishers Since 2012

Published by Lyfe Publishing LLC

Lyfe Publishing, 10800 Nautica Place, White Plains MD 20695

Library of Congress Cataloging in Publications Data

Gerald C. Anderson, Sr.

Love & Lust / Gerald C. Anderson, Sr.

ISBN: 978-1-957333-18-2

(Fictitious Character)-Fiction

Panama City, Florida

Love & Lust–Fiction

Printed in the United States of America

1 2 3 4 5 6 7 8 9 10

Book design by Olivia Pro Designs and Lyfe Designs

Editor

Beryl Anthony Brackett

Chief Editor

BAB Productions, LLC

18103 Merino Drive

Accokeek, Maryland 20607

DEDICATION

Tyndall AFB, FL, was one of my favorite assignments in the Air Force. I've always wanted to write a story using the city and base as a backdrop. This novella fits perfectly. The people of Panama City were great, and it was truly an honor serving there. Love you Panama City!

ACKNOWLEDGEMENT

Thank you for your support with "Love & Lust"

Beryl Brackett

Danyelle Woodson

Danny Sells

Also, By Gerald C. Anderson, Sr.

We Come in Peace

27 Hours

Standing Firm

Secrets

The Last Song

The Lawyer

Saved

The Room

Are You Innocent?

The Compendium Series

Weight Loss

Warlord

The Last Honorable Man

The Dream

The Death Knights

Twins

The Ride Along

Creative Inspirations

Fatal Misperceptions

Prologue

The Tyndall Air Force Base basketball team faced its toughest challenge of the season. The championship game was in its final moments, and they were down by two points.

Jonathan Rose was the team's best player. Jonathan was considered by many to be headed to a division one college before an injury prevented him from going. He enlisted in the Air Force instead and now leads his team in scoring.

Two seconds were on the clock, and Terrance in bounded the ball to Jonathan. Jonathan took the ball, made a quick move to get free and shot the three pointer.

It was all net! Tyndall won the Southern Region championship game and brought home the Commander's Trophy for the first time in 20 years.

After the game, Jonathan, Terrance and their friend Ed were at the NCO Club celebrating. Every woman on the base wanted to be with Jonathan, but he had his eye on one in particular. Terrance said, "Man, you have Donna. Why are you trying to get with Simone? I saw her first."

"Dude, she doesn't like you and you know it, but I'm going to hit that tonight." Jonathan sipped his drink and walked over to Simone, who stood with her friends. He said, "Hello, Simone. How are you tonight?"

"I'm good Mr. Superstar. Where's your ball and chain?"

"We're not married, you know."

"I know, but she is my friend."

"Is that going to stop us from going back to your room?"

"Jonathan Rose, are you putting the moves on me?"

"I am."

She smiled at him seductively, "What about your boys? You know they both want me. What should I tell them? Oh, and they don't have girlfriends or kids like you do."

"Well, it's up to you. Just so you know, Donna isn't here because I'm leaving her. I'm sure she told you by now."

"Me and Donna aren't the best of friends. We tolerate each other because Erica is our mutual friend. If she were breaking up with you, she wouldn't tell me."

"I'm telling you. How about we shoot over to your room and finish this conversation?"

"Look at your boys."

Jonathan glanced over at Terrance and Ed. They both held drinks in their hands and watched his every move. He giggled inside, knowing they admired him, "What about them?"

"You really don't care that they wanted me first?"

"Actually, no I don't. If you wanted them, you would have had them; but you want me as much as I want you. Am I right?"

"Maybe." She looked him in the eyes and stroked his chin, "I hope you're not lying to me Jonathan Rose."

He looked her up and down. The fire red dress fit tightly against her hourglass shaped body. Every woman in the club wanted Jonathan for his stardom on the court, but every man wanted Simone for her appearance. "Let's go baby." He gently took her arm and guided her out of the club. He knew he had every man's admiration as he walked out with the prettiest woman in the club.

Jonathan waved at his boys. He never noticed the anger in their eyes.

Chapter 1

Jonathan Rose struggled to get out of bed. It was the roughest night of his young life. His boys threw him a bachelor party to end all parties, and he drank more than he ever expected. He looked beside him in shock. It was the beautiful woman who popped out of his cake. Everyone in the room marveled at her caramel skin tone. She was the perfect five foot seven for his height. He slapped his forehead. *"Wow, I can't believe I did this on the eve of my wedding. Donna is going to kill me if she finds out!"*

Terrance and Ed burst into the room. Jonathan shouted, "We got to get her out of here, man! If Donna finds out, she will kill me." The two friends laughed, and Casey woke up. Jonathan continued, "Dude, we got to get her out of her. Donna's dad is on the way."

Terrance said, "Okay man, but there's something you should know."

"What's that?"

"You didn't have sex with her. We just put her in the bed with you."

Jonathan frowned, "I could punch both of you right now."

Casey said, "Where's my money?"

Jonathan replied, "Yeah, pay her. You got your laugh, and it's time to pay for it." Terrance paid Casey. She grabbed her clothes and left the apartment. Jonathan continued, "I can't believe you two did this to me."

Ed responded, "You needed to have some fun before you get tied down forever."

"Very funny but being with Donna is not a prison sentence. It's a reward."

Ed continued, "Yeah, whatever you say, dude. Now let's get in these monkey suits. One of Donna's friends might want some tonight."

Terrence said, "Yeah, there's a desperate one in the group all the time."

Ed replied, "You got jokes."

Jonathan sat on the edge of the bed while his two best friends left the room. This was the day he long awaited. Donna was the woman of his dreams. Her tall, slim chocolate covered body excited him every time she came near. From the day he met her, he was in love. She got pregnant from the first time they were together. His gorgeous twin girls, Chloe, and Zoe were the splitting image of their mother.

The sound of the door opening alerted him that his future father-in-law arrived. Earl walked into the suite bedroom. Jonathan stood up, expecting a challenge. He got it. Earl said, "This is the day I've dreaded for a while now. Let's get something straight; I don't want you to be my son-in-law. I think you're a cheater and you'll always be one. You are the father of my granddaughters, and I don't know what my daughter sees in you. I can't change that. If I catch you cheating on Donna, it will be the end for you. Do we understand each other?"

"Yes, sir." Earl turned and walked out the room. Terrance and Ed laughed at Jonathan, but Jonathan did not laugh. He hated Earl, but some things he said were true. Jonathan's lust for women was strong and he had issues controlling it.

Jonathan stood at the altar waiting for Donna to arrive. Slowly, the bridesmaids and groomsmen made their way down the aisle to the front of the church. Now that moment, everyone loved arrived. She stood at the end of the church directly in front of him in a gorgeous white gown. Standing by their godmother, Erica, were Chloe and Zoe, having laid the flowers on the path for Donna to walk on. Beside him was his best man, Terrance, and his nephew, JJ, who carried the rings to the altar.

The music changed, and everyone stood. She walked slowly down the aisle with her dad by her side. Jonathan loved every step. No woman in the world could match her. She was the epitome of love. This was a day he would always remember. The day he fell in love a thousand times with his wife.

After the wedding and reception, Jonathan laid in the honeymoon suite of one of New York City's finest hotels. Their military friends paid for them to stay there for part of their honeymoon. His cell rang, and he answered, "Terrance, dude, are you really calling me on my honeymoon night?"

"Dude, how many times have you hit that? Look, there's a sweet honey at the bar asking about you."

"Asking about me? Why?"

"Dude, it's Simone, and she is hot." He laughed, "As she usually is, I might add."

"Simone? What's Donna's friend, or used to be her friend, doing here?"

"She was in town, heard about the wedding, and said it should have been her."

"Man, she was so good, but Donna gave me an ultimatum."

Terrance said, "Man, she was fine back then and still fine now."

"Yeah, she is. Hey, when Donna falls asleep, I'm going down there to chat with her. Maybe..." Donna came out of the bathroom. "Hey, man, stop interrupting me and my new bride!" Jonathan hung up the phone. "Hey, baby, I love that sexy black nightgown. Come on over her and take care of your man."

Donna smiled and leaned into him, "Yes, baby, I can do that!"

Afterwards Jonathan laid down beside his beautiful bride, proud of his work. He slipped out of bed and got dressed. It was one in the morning, so he hoped Simone would still be in the bar. Jonathan eased out of the suite and headed downstairs. "*What lie will I tell if I get caught... hmm, it has to be a good!*"

The elevator reached the lobby, and Jonathan headed to the bar. It was still open, so he celebrated that minor victory. He walked inside and there was Simone sitting at the bar with Terrance. He hoped Terrance was not trying to put the moves on her. Terrance liked

Simone first years ago, but they got over the fact that Jonathan took her. "Well, look who's in town."

"Hello, Jonathan. How are you?"

"I'm doing well."

"I bet you are. According to your friend here, you married Donna today. How is she?"

"Sleeping right now, but fine."

"And the children?"

"They are doing well. Can we take this conversation to a booth?"

Simone smiled, "Honey, you're married and this single man here, Terrance, has got me stirred up. I probably should have dated him instead of you."

Jonathan looked at his boy and frowned. Terrance interjected, "Hey, be it far from me to interfere in this reunion."

Terrance walked away. Jonathan continued, "See, he's gone. Now can we make our way to that booth?" Simone stood and Jonathan bit his tongue. She wore her tight dress like no other. The color accented her skin tone and sparked excitement in Jonathan. One look at her and he forgot his love and dedication to Donna.

Jonathan guided her to a booth in the back, hoping none of Donna's family or friends would see them. "Now, this is better."

Simone said, "It's better because you can keep me in the shadows again."

"Come on, baby, you know how I feel about you."

"Jonathan, you feel horny about me and that's about it. All you want from me is sex. I don't understand why, because all Donna did was brag about how good you made her feel."

Jonathan smiled, "I made you feel good too, right?"

Simone rolled her eyes at him. She looked at her watch and said, "I have an early flight back to Panama City. I'll see you around."

"You're stationed at Tyndall again?"

"Yes, I'm a glutton for punishment, I guess. Bye."

"Wait, wait... come on, let's have a drink."

Simone sighed, "What are you expecting? You just got married a few hours ago. Now, you come down here at one in the morning expecting for me to jump in the bed with you after you've had sex with Donna? Are you serious, dude?" She stood up and continued, "If I had something to drink in front of me, I'd throw in your face."

Jonathan was disappointed. He wanted her to jump in the bed with him. The memories of their times together flooded his mind. Terrance joined him in the booth. "Dude, you better get upstairs before Donna wakes up."

"Yeah, I wanted that so bad."

"You had your wife; your new wife."

"We're all dogs, Terrance. Even when I try to be good, I can't help but be bad. They like it when I'm bad."

"True, which is why I don't understand why you got married."

"The kids."

"That makes sense, bro. So, she's gone?"

Jonathan's sadness was evident, "Yeah, she cursed me out without saying one curse word and left. I really liked her."

Terrance sighed, "So, if you didn't have the kids, you would have married Simone?"

"I wouldn't go that far, but I really liked the sex. When I was at that wedding, I seriously thought I loved Donna, but I don't know man. Seeing Simone again makes me think I was in love with the idea of marriage, not Donna. In a few minutes, I was ready to cheat again."

Terrance laughed, "Oh, I got you. Go upstairs and get laid again. You'll forget all about any of this."

"You're right. Let me go wake my wife up."

Terrance laughed, and Jonathan went back upstairs. When he returned, it was not the reception he hoped. Donna sat on the bed with her legs crossed. She frowned at him the instant he walked into the bedroom portion of the suite. He realized he was in deep trouble. *"Dang and I didn't even get any!"*

Jonathan sighed, "Um… hey, baby."

"Don't hey baby me. On our wedding night, Jonathan? How could you?"

"All I did was go down to the bar. What's the big deal?"

"The big deal is that you were not here when I rolled over. Given your history, what do you think I suspect you were doing? I would bet all the tea in China you were trying to hit on some woman. You have me, your wife, all alone in this suite and you'd rather be downstairs in the bar? I must be crazy for marrying you."

Jonathan thought, *"You're not the only one who feels that way right about now. This will turn into a three-hour sermon. I'd rather be in church."* "I was only in the bar talking to Terrance. You were asleep and I couldn't sleep. Again, I say, what's the big deal?"

"There is no big deal, Jonathan." She stormed out of the bedroom. Through all the conversation,

12

Jonathan never noticed she was fully dressed. The sound of the suite's door closing got his attention.

"Hey, where are you going?" He rushed to the door. Donna was getting on the elevator. Jonathan shouted, "Where are you going?" Donna let the doors close without answering his question. Jonathan thought, *"Well, she has to come back to get her luggage."*

He returned to the suite and sat on the couch. *"How long will she stay out? She's got to be in one of her girl's rooms. I'll give it a few, then call."* A few turned into hours. When Jonathan woke, it was seven in the morning and Donna had not returned. He went into the bedroom to wash up. He noticed all of Donna's luggage was gone. *"Wow, she planned to leave me when I returned. This is embarrassing. I need to find my wife."*

After he washed up, Jonathan called Donna's friends. None of them would share her whereabouts with him. He called Donna's mom and got an earful from her. He quickly regretted calling her. At the end of the sermon, she refused to tell him anything. For the first time, Jonathan regretted his actions. *"If I get her back, I promise I won't cheat again."* He heard the front door opening. *"Thank you, Jesus."* He rushed into the living room area and smiled. Donna's face did not reciprocate.

Donna said, "You cheated on me for the last time. Tomorrow morning, I am going to get a lawyer and undo this marriage. Hopefully, it can be annulled."

"Baby, don't do that. Please, I promise I didn't cheat last night, and I will never cheat again. The boys tried to get me to do something Friday night, but I didn't. Please, one more chance, Donna."

Donna sat down on the couch, "You didn't go down to the bar to talk to Terrance. You went down there to talk to Simone. Who do you think contacted me? The call woke me up, and I was told you were on the prowl."

There was nothing Jonathan could say. She had him dead to rights. He never believed Simone would turn on him and tell Donna about the attempt to sleep with her again. There was a line even he thought she would not cross. He continued to beg, "Okay, complete transparency. I went down there to talk with her, but we didn't connect because I didn't want to. She was in the hotel where we were staying and I wanted to know why. I was trying to protect you."

"You're lying again."

"No, I'm not. I don't know what she told you, but that's the truth, baby; I swear."

She studied him as she often did. Inside, he prayed he would get another chance. He promised himself he would make good on it. He could see in her eyes she was thinking about it. She popped up, "One more chance for the sake of the kids. If you screw this up, Jonathan, I swear I will leave you forever. Do you understand me?"

"Yes, baby, I clearly understand."

She walked toward him. He readied himself for the makeup kiss, but it did not come. She walked past him into the bedroom area. He quickly followed, hoping to makeup with a round of sex. He placed his hands on her hips from behind, but she removed them and turned toward him. "I said, one more chance but sex… that's out of question for now. We need to get packed to make it to our cruise ship."

That wasn't what he wanted to hear, but he would go with it. Donna put Jonathan in the doghouse on other occasions so this would not be the first, but he hoped he could restrain himself and make his marriage last.

They arrived at the cruise ship and processed onto the ship. Jonathan was excited. He looked around without giving Donna reason to know he was looking. The number of single women on the ship made him salivate. He said, "Baby, this honeymoon will be the start of making everything right with you. I love you more than you know." He thought, *"God, I need to stop lying. I thought I loved you but after seeing Simone… whoa, baby, the beast is loose again!"*

Donna broke his thoughts, "I don't doubt your love for me, Jonathan. I doubt your ability to stay faithful to me. In fact, I doubt your ability to stay faithful to anyone." She turned and looked him in the eye. "I only married you because of our children. I always wanted my kids to have both parents in the house with them. I thought you would be faithful. I thought if you had a reason to be loyal, it would be for your family. I know you see a lot of pretty girls and after having your children, I don't have the same figure I used to have, but you will grow tired of them like you have me."

"I haven't grown tired of you, baby. You will see; I will be loyal." He knew his statements were not true. His lust for women was out of control again and he knew it, but he could not stop it. He did not want to stop it. He wanted sex, and he wanted it from multiple women.

Donna said, "I think you should talk to someone when we get back."

Jonathan thought, *"Oh, my goodness. She can't be serious. I've got to change the course of this conversation. Oh wow, look at that honey over there. She looks like Simone. Boy, I know I have a thing for them redbones."*

His thoughts were so locked into the woman he lusted for that he did not hear Donna's words. She pinched him, "Are you listening to me?" She looked around, "I knew it. I'm so out of here!"

"Wait, I wasn't looking at anyone. I was thinking about what you were saying." Donna stopped and looked at him. "I know it looked like I was looking at her, but I was thinking. My eyes were in that direction, but I was thinking about going to see someone." She appeared to calm down, "If you want me to go talk to someone, then I will."

"Okay, let's get to our room before they start that exercise."

"Sure." *"I can't believe that 'I'm thinking' line worked. Wow, that redbone was hot. I got to get that number before I get off this ship."* They made it to their cabin and Jonathan loved it. "This room is awesome. Baby, you know we have some great friends and family. They did all this for us."

"I know, right. Our friends are the bomb. Look, I'm sorry to be so hard on you, but you've got to see what we can have here. We're both young and at the start of our military careers. We can grow together in this world personally and professionally, but we must be on the same page."

"I am on the same page as you, honey. We're going to do this. I will win back your trust."

Donna popped her lips, "I hope so."

The exercise drill came and went with no fanfare. Jonathan and Donna got dressed for dinner with the captain that evening. When they arrived, Jonathan felt they were the best dressed couple in the dining area. The host sat them at their table. Jonathan ordered drinks for them. He said, "Baby, this is so nice.

Coming on this cruise was a brilliant idea. I'm glad I had it."

"Excuse me? You need to stop lying."

They both laughed. Jonathan's jaw dropped when the couple they were to share the table with arrived. It was the redbone girl he saw earlier. *"Oh, my. I can't believe it. Who is this dude she's with?"*

The couple took their seats and introduced themselves. "Hi, I'm Ray and this is my wife Vanessa."

Jonathan said, "I'm Jonathan, and this is my beautiful wife, Donna."

Ray replied, "It's good to meet you guys. We're on our second honeymoon. How about you?"

Jonathan smiled, "We're newlyweds."

Vanessa said, "What? Congratulations. You guys are us from a year ago. We came on this cruise after our wedding. We loved it and it started our marriage off the right way."

Donna cut her eyes at Jonathan and said, "We're hoping for the same thing for us."

Jonathan replied, "It will be, baby."

The couples made small talk through the evening. Jonathan did his best to keep his eyes off Vanessa. He thought, *"She won't be easy to get to. She's all in love and everything, living in Tennessee. I guess I'll have to set my*

GERALD C. ANDERSON, SR.

sights elsewhere." The ladies left for the ladies' room, leaving Jonathan and Ray alone.

Ray said, "Whew, I thought they would never leave. No offense to your wife, man, but I was growing tired of mine."

"What? I thought you guys were happily married."

"She is; I'm not. I've had my eye on those twins over there. Are you checking them out?"

"No, man, where?"

"Look to your right and back about ten feet."

Jonathan smiled, "Wow, they are hot."

"Man, I should have left my ball and chain at home and came on this cruise with my boys. I saw those twins in their swimsuits earlier. Dude, let me tell you! I was trying to control myself."

"Man, I wish I would have seen that. I hear there's a club on the ship. Maybe we can leave the wives in the rooms and hit the club."

Ray rubbed his hands together, "Sounds like a plan, my man."

The ladies returned and Jonathan was excited to have a new friend like his boys, Terrance and Ed. The cruise would be even better if he could get time away from his wife.

The couples finished their dinner and headed out. The ladies agreed to change and meet in the club. Jonathan hoped they would hang out for a while, then retire to their rooms without the men. Then he could go on the prowl with his new friend.

Donna came out of the bathroom in a tight blue dress. Jonathan thought, *"Man, those twins put a little something on her stomach."*

"Jonathan, how do I look? Does this dress fit me?"

"No, not like Simone." "Yeah, baby, it's fine." *"It doesn't matter. I'm not going to the club for you anyway."* Jonathan smiled, "Let's do this."

They headed out of their cabin and to the club. Ray and Vanessa were waiting for them to arrive. Ray gave Jonathan that nod, so they both knew they were on the same page. They wanted the wives to leave early.

Vanessa said, "Donna girl, you look amazing!"

Jonathan thought, *"No baby, you look amazing! I don't know why my boy doesn't love you anymore, but if I had you, I'd love you forever!"* Jonathan said, "Hey, let's grab that table and order some drinks." They all walked over to the table Jonathan selected and took a seat. Ray tapped Jonathan on the arm. He looked up and noticed the twins coming into the club. They had to get rid of the women, for sure.

Midnight on the ocean settled in for the couples. Jonathan prayed Donna would want to go back to the room without him. She said, "Jonathan, I'm tired."

Jonathan answered with excitement, "Okay, do you mind if I hang out with Ray for a little while? We're talking about doing a recording or two down the road."

Donna looked into his eyes. She knew he loved playing the piano and music was his thing. It was perfect that Ray played the bass. They could use the deception to be alone. Donna replied, "I'm tired and I want us to go to our cabin."

"Dang it! I knew she would go there." Jonathan looked Ray in the eyes, "Maybe tomorrow, man."

"No worries. Me and Vanessa are headed back to our cabin too."

Jonathan realized Vanessa was putting the same pressure on him. He recognized he would have to play the game longer than he expected, but he hoped the time would come when he would get a kitchen pass. Then he would use it to his advantage.

The morning sun rose, and Donna was up early. She wanted to explore the ship in more detail. Jonathan wanted to sleep in, but she would not let him out of her sight. *"This has got to end. I can't be followed around like this. I need my freedom."* He looked into the bathroom mirror and did not like the man looking back. Part of him understood he was wrong for the way he thought and treated Donna. Inside, he knew she was a great woman who deserved a loyal man. That man, however, was not him. *"I'm only 22 years old. I don't need to be tied down to one woman. What was I thinking?"*

He stepped out of the bathroom to a waiting Donna. Her arms were folded, which never meant anything good for Jonathan. In the two years they dated, he learned many of her mannerism. Folded arms were never good. "Are you ready, dude?"

"Why do you always call me dude? What happened to my pet names?"

"Ask Simone."

He ended that line of questioning, knowing it would only lead to a sermon about infidelity. A sermon he was tired of hearing. He was who he was, and he was not going to change.

They walked out and explored the ship. The couple agreed to meet Ray and Vanessa at noon for lunch. Jonathan noticed Donna and Vanessa were becoming fast friends. He remembered how close she was to Simone, but he was able to have an affair with her. Maybe it would be the same with Vanessa except they lived in Tennessee while Jonathan and Donna lived in Panama City, Florida. He rationalized he needed it once. That would be enough for him.

The noon hour arrived. Jonathan and Donna met with Ray and Vanessa. They had fun again. Jonathan enjoyed Ray's company. He knew if they were living in the same city, they would be friends like his boys. The wives went shopping and insisted on their husbands join them. This time, the men could talk while the ladies went into the stores. Jonathan asked Ray, "Man, why do you think we cheat?"

"It's inbred in us. We are the hunters, and we can't just hunt once and quit. We try but we can't do it. None of the men I know are truly loyal to their wives."

"None of my friends are either."

"Look, Jonathan, it's coded in our DNA. We see something we like and man, we have to go for it. Those twins have been on my mind since I saw them yesterday. I got to go for it."

"Dude, if your wife catches you…"

"I know. She puts up a front telling everyone we're the perfect couple, but man, we are far from perfect. When I'm at home in Memphis, I'm on the prowl every weekend. I haven't had sex with my wife in a couple of months."

Jonathan thought that was insane. If he had a chance, he'd knock that out in a minute. "What? Man, how do you do that?"

"You're a newlywed man. Wait till you've been married a while. Same old repetitive sex. She doesn't want to try new things. In a word... boring."

Jonathan could not believe his ears. To him, Vanessa was fine, and he wanted it bad. He hid it well from his new friend. "It's amazing how you don't know what someone is like until you've been with them. When I see your wife, I think Ray is a lucky man. But hearing you, Ray isn't so lucky at all."

"No, man. Ray isn't lucky. Now you and Donna... oh man, she's hot."

"What? Do you see her gut? Having those twins did a number on her man. I still hit it every chance I get, but it's not like it used to be."

"Dude, check your eyesight, bro. Your wife is fine."

Jonathan could not believe his ears. Was he overlooking how beautiful his wife still was? Had he grown complacent with her figure? He looked at her in the store and thought, *"You know, maybe I have a fine wife and I should focus on her more."*

Ray continued, "Yo look, it's the twins. I got to get into a conversation with them. Help me out."

"Yeah, if I want to sleep in the cafeteria tonight."

They both laughed. The twins came near them, and Ray struck up a conversation with one of them.

Jonathan watched. Keeping one eye on Donna and listening to the conversation Ray had with them. Finally, Ray asked for one of the twin's numbers. She responded with questioning him about Vanessa. Jonathan admired Ray's boldness to hit on the twins while his wife was in the next room. He also admired his ability to lie at the drop of a hat. He was better than him at the game. Ray convinced Mia that his marriage was on its last leg and wanted to start something with her even though she lived in Washington, DC.

Ray motioned for Jonathan to get Lea's number. Jonathan loved the thought of getting with her, but he held back. He knew Donna watched. Before the wives came out of the store. Donna rolled her eyes at him and pulled him to the side. She asked, "Empty your pockets."

Jonathan thought she was crazy. "Are you serious?"

"You've cheated on me too many times. If you got that girl's number, I will catch a plane from Jamaica back to Panama City and divorce you."

Jonathan showed her what he had in his pockets. "See, you owe me an apology."

"This time maybe, but not for all the other times you've cheated on me."

"You're right, but I told you, I'm done with that life. I'm all about you." Donna rolled her eyes and walked back to Ray and Vanessa.

Vanessa asked, "Is everything okay?"

Donna answered, "Yes, we're good… this time." She looked at Jonathan. He thanked God he resisted getting Lea's number but wondered why Vanessa did not question her husband.

The couples continued to shop, but the wives no longer let their husbands stand in the hallway. They both insisted they come into the store as well. Jonathan grew tired of following her around. He grew tired of her and her reluctance to trust him. They walked past the chapel and the chaplain was cleaning the window. Donna said, "Hi, sir. Are you busy? I mean, besides the obvious." She laughed, and the chaplain chuckled as well.

"I always have time for those who want to hear the word of God."

Jonathan could not believe it. She stopped to go to church. He had to get off this merry-go-round. He needed to get away and get a drink. Most of all, he needed to be hunting for someone new to be with. Donna pulled him away from his thoughts. She said, "This is my husband, Jonathan. I love him so much, but he has a problem that he won't acknowledge. Can you talk to him?"

Jonathan's anger welled up inside. *"I know she didn't just put me on the spot like this! It's on now. No more respect. I'm going to find me someone to spend this cruise with!"* The chaplain looked at Jonathan. Before he could say anything, Jonathan said, "I don't need to talk to him. I told you I was fine and I'm not about that life anymore. Why are you putting me on blast like this?" Without waiting for a response, he walked away.

He did not realize how far he walked away from Donna, but his anger was stronger than he realized. He even considered cutting his ties and leaving the woman he married. Jonathan sat down next to the pool and watched the kids playing. He thought about his own children and wondered what they were doing. Leaving Donna would mean leaving his children. He loved them and given their military circumstances, he would have issues seeing his children if he got a divorce. The thought of her getting an assignment different from him could mean years and an outrageous amount of expenses to see his children. *"It's cheaper to keep her for sure. Especially since I love my kids so much."*

Donna tracked him down. Ray and Vanessa were not in sight. She eased down beside him and put her hand on top of his hand. "I'm sorry for that. I just want to be sure you're past this cheating thing. Do you know how it made me feel to find out you went downstairs to be with Simone again? Do you know the pain I have inside each time you cheat on me?"

He looked at her, and the pain was etched into her eyes. He said, "I realize I've hurt you, Donna, and that's why I say that life is behind me. Give me a chance."

She stood up, "You got it. I'm going to stop treating you like I don't trust you. Now it's up to you to prove your loyalty to me."

"I will." The couple smiled and hugged. Jonathan was not sure if he could really be loyal, but for now, things with them were good. Maybe they would stay that way.

Chapter 2

Evening came, and the men arrived at the club. The ladies were attending an event for women. Donna wanted to hear the guest speaker on women's empowerment. She also pressed Jonathan about attending a couple's event on marriage the next evening. Jonathan had a day to figure out a reason not to go, but realized in the end she would likely win.

It was Jonathan's time to test his loyalty. Ray looked around like he was looking for someone. Jonathan asked, "Who are you looking for?"

"Mia. She said she would be here." He looked at his watch. Jonathan pointed to the door. Ray continued, "There's my baby."

Jonathan said, "Dude, what if your wife comes in?"

"They will be at that event until ten. We got two hours. I'm going to get me some."

Jonathan smiled at the twins. Mia said, "Hi guys, how are you?"

Ray said, "I'm good. My friend here is a little nervous. Maybe your sister can help him with that." Ray looked at Jonathan, "See you later bro." They walked away, leaving Jonathan with Lea.

Beads of sweat raced down Jonathan's back. He repaired the damage to his marriage, and now he was back in a situation where he honestly hoped he would not be. *I can't believe the temptation. She is so hot and I'm actually trying to do right. Well, maybe not trying that hard. If there's a God, why are you tempting me like this?*

"Are you okay?"

Jonathan did not hear her voice. Instead, he imagined Donna walking into the club and dumping him on the spot. She asked again, "Hey, are you good?"

"Um, yeah… yeah, I'm fine. How are you?"

"I'm good and a little thirsty."

"Okay, let me get you a drink."

"Thank you…"

Jonathan said, "Sorry, I'm a little nervous."

"It's okay. I know you're married."

"Yeah, but that didn't seem to stop your sister."

"No, it doesn't. We are of the philosophy that everyone cheats. Relax. We can just sit here and enjoy the evening. I'm okay either way."

Jonathan could not believe his ears. This woman believed in cheating as much as he does but for once he wanted to do right. Donna trusted him and he needed to reward that trust, but Lea was so pretty. *"I have to resist. I just have to!"* Jonathan asked, "So you believe everyone cheats in their relationship or marriage?"

"I do. Personally, I can have guilt free sex."

"Guilt free sex? I didn't know that was a thing."

"It is, and I'm sure you've experienced it. Tell me you haven't had sex with someone behind your significant others' back and not felt guilty about it."

"Okay, I see your point."

Lea smiled, and Jonathan's heart lit up. He imagined taking her back to her room for a little pleasure. *"Donna wouldn't find out about it. This woman is just in it for a little sex and nothing more. Why not? I can be faithful tomorrow."* He asked, "So if we were to explore this guilt free sex a little further, where would we go?"

"To my cabin. Me and my sister paid for single occupancy so we could have some privacy."

"Wow, that sounds expensive."

"We saved up for it. This is our annual vacation. We come on a cruise hoping to get lucky, but we don't want to go home with anyone. Too many issues after you leave the ship."

"Really?"

"Yeah, the first year I was here, I met this guy. He was hot, and I was into him, but again, I only wanted some entertainment while I was on board. He slipped away from his wife a few nights and we had some fun. Afterwards, he wanted to divorce his wife and marry me. I can't have that on my conscience. I can have guilt free sex, but I would feel guilty if I broke up someone's marriage."

"Hmm, that's a lot to take in, but where's your cabin?"

Lea laughed, "Are you sure you want to go down this road, baby?"

"I'm thinking about it."

"Well, it looks like it will have to be another night. There's your ball and chain."

"Oh, no. She's going to lose her mind."

Donna and Vanessa came over to Jonathan and Lea. Donna said, "Jonathan?"

"Hey, babe. This is Lea. I don't know where her twin sister is, but they come onboard every year for their vacation. Lea, this is my beautiful wife, Donna."

Lea said, "It's nice to meet you."

Donna replied, "It's nice to meet you too. We saw you both at the dinner last night."

"Yeah, that food was so good."

Ray and Mia walked up. Vanessa rolled her eyes at Ray, "Where have you been?"

"I showed Mia where the bowling alley was. She wanted to go bowling tonight with her sister."

Mia added, "Yeah, are you ready, Lea?"

"Yep." Lea looked at Jonathan, "This is our annual event too. She thinks she's going to win tonight."

Jonathan laughed, and the twins walked away. Donna looked him in the eye and Jonathan said, "Don't go there. You saw me at the bar, having a conversation, and that's all."

"I'm not saying a word or jumping to conclusions."

Vanessa said, "Well, I am! I know you were doing more than showing that heifer where the bowling alley was, Ray. I'm ready to go back to our cabin... now Ray!"

Ray answered, "See you guys later."

They walked off, leaving Jonathan and Donna. Jonathan asked, "Do you want a drink?"

"Sure. I'm trusting you, Jonathan. Don't make me regret it." They enjoyed a couple of drinks and worked their way up to laughing. After Donna got over the issue with Lea, they had an enjoyable time.

After the club, Jonathan and Donna returned to their cabin. Jonathan dressed and got in the bed. Donna was in the bathroom, as usual. This was often their routine and Jonathan became accustomed to it. She walked out of the bathroom in that nicely fitted nightgown that Jonathan adored. It showed every curve on her body. He realized Ray was right. He had forgotten how fine she truly was. She laid down on the bed flat on her back, inviting Jonathan to get on top of her. He accepted the invitation and asked, "I thought I was in the doghouse."

"You were, but you've done well and… I'm horny. No sense punishing myself."

Jonathan smiled and kissed her sensual lips. He made his way down her soft body to the place he loved the most. He knew she loved it, too.

The night rolled by with Jonathan enjoying every moment. He questioned how he could even think of cheating on Donna.

The morning of the third day on board, the ship arrived. This was the day they would go into Jamaica and sightsee. Jonathan rose and washed up. He wanted to hit the gym first while Donna slept. As he headed for the door, she asked, "Where are you going?"

"I thought you were asleep. I'm going to get a workout in before we disembark."

"Okay, don't be too long."

"I won't." He headed out of the room and toward the gym. He thought, "Wow, she didn't even question my going to the gym. I think I'm good now." Lea walked out her room in a bikini that screamed at Jonathan. He swallowed hard and said, "Oh, lawd! Girl, you look awesome."

Lea winked her eye at him. "Where are you headed?"

"To the gym."

"I'm going down by the pool. I didn't get any action last night so, I figured I would go for a swim."

"You… didn't get any action?"

"Nope. There were some guys interested, but I wasn't interested in them. How long does your wife let you go to the gym?"

"Usually a couple of hours."

"Do you want to come inside my cabin?" Jonathan's mouth watered. He won back the favor of his wife and enjoyed a great night with her, but the sex was routine. Donna never strayed away from the usual.

Jonathan could not pass up this beautiful woman. She was pretty and had a body that was irresistible. She put her hand on his chest, "Jonathan, I'm insatiable right now. I need something."

Jonathan felt the beads of sweat roll down his back again. This time it was not nerves, it was lust taking over his body, his every sensation. He said, "Lead the way." They walked inside Lea's room and Jonathan broke the vows of his marriage. In the past, he cheated on Donna as her boyfriend. Now, after he won her trust back, he could not stop himself from breaking his vows of marriage.

Chapter 3

Jonathan, Donna, Ray and Vanessa disembarked the cruise ship to do some sightseeing and shopping. Jonathan relished the thoughts of his morning. He had a great night with his bride and topped it off with a little something extra from Lea. He wanted to tell Ray about it, but he needed to wait until the ladies were out of earshot. When they stumbled upon the crystal shop, he got his chance. Donna loved crystal objects, and their duplex in Panama City was filled with them.

Jonathan and Ray sat outside the shop with drinks while the ladies went inside. Jonathan asked, "How long are you in the doghouse?"

"Dude, why they had to come back early last night? Man, now I probably won't get to hit that."

"Bro, I hit it."

Ray's hand covered his mouth, "Whoa, you lying? When?"

"This morning, man. I was on my way to the gym, and Lea came out of her room in this fire red bikini suit. Oh lawd, she was extremely hot. Check this. She asked me to come in and hit it."

"Yeah, man, they're a strange breed. They believe in guilt free sex. I'm all in."

Jonathan laughed, "I know. I can't believe she said that. We need more women like that in this world."

"Tell me about it. Jonathan man, you need to run interference for me while I get with Mia. I can't miss out on that."

"I got you, bro. Let's come up with a plan. Hey, I know… go to the gym with me in the morning. You'll get two uninterrupted hours with Mia."

"I'm in, dude. I will tell Vanessa you and I are going to the gym. We'll meet the girls in their rooms and have a good time."

Jonathan replied, "You got it. Hey, here they come. Looks like my wife stacked up. More crystal around the dang apartment."

Ray said, "She said she loves them."

"That she does, bro… that she does." The ladies joined them at their table. Jonathan asked, "Do we have any money left, honey?"

Donna giggled, "Of course we do. We have my paycheck. Yours is gone." They all laughed. Inside, Jonathan was relieved. Donna had no idea what he did that morning, and he planned to keep it that way. With any luck, he would have a couple more mornings with Lea.

Walking toward them were the twins. Jonathan got excited but nervous too. How would Lea react? Would she truly be the guilt free sex person she said she was? He was about to find out. Mia and Lea stopped. Lea said, "Hey, you guys enjoying the sights and shops?"

Donna answered, "You can tell by my bag I'm enjoying the shops for sure."

Lea laughed and replied, "I see. Well, we're headed to the beach to soak up this sun. See y'all at dinner."

Donna replied, "Bye." Vanessa did not say anything. The anger wore on her face. Jonathan noticed Ray made no contact with Mia and Mia kept to herself. It was obvious there was tension between them. Donna continued, "Are you okay, Vanessa?"

"I'm okay, but what's the punishment for murder?"

Ray replied, "Come on baby, stop it. Nothing happened. All I did was show her where the bowling alley was."

Vanessa replied, "Do you think I'm stupid? If they're bowling on this ship every year, then how she doesn't know where it is?"

Jonathan said, "Different ship maybe?"

Ray added, "Right! They never said it was the same ship. They probably go to a different place every year."

Donna said, "Okay, Vanessa, that make sense. I wouldn't want to come to the same place every year." She looked at Jonathan, "Stay out of it, honey."

Vanessa popped her lips, "Yeah, well, I still don't trust my husband."

Donna said, "I don't blame you. Mine just got out of the doghouse. Hey, let's grab some authentic Jamaican food."

Jonathan said, "I thought you told me to stay out of it?"

"I told you that." She pinched his cheeks.

The group headed to get some food. Jonathan could not wait for the day to end and morning to come so he could be with Lea again. They made an agreement to meet at six in the morning for round two.

Jonathan's evening and night went according to plan. They dined with Ray and Vanessa, then they all went to the club. Jonathan stayed away from Lea in the club, but it frustrated him at the sight of her with another man. He hoped she was just spending time with him and nothing more. After seeing them leave together, Jonathan grew angrier inside. He wondered if he loved her and, if he did, did he love her more than he loved his wife?

After Jonathan and Donna returned to their cabin, Jonathan planned to sneak out and go to Lea's room. Donna asked, "Are you okay?"

"Yeah, I'm just tired."

"You seemed upset all evening. Did I do anything to you?"

"No, baby, not at all. It's just been a long day. I think I'm going to retire."

"Wow, you must be tired."

Jonathan forced himself to lie. "I am, baby. I know you want to do something, but can I get a raincheck?" He could not believe he was passing on sex with Donna. Having sex with her was not the greatest of experiences and she did not get insatiable often, but when she did, it was far better. Jonathan could not get his mind off Lea. *What did she do to me?*

Before long, Donna was asleep. Jonathan laid next to her, wondering if he could get out of the room and go to Lea's room. He was desperate to know if she was alone. If she was, what would he do then? If Donna caught him cheating, she would leave him. *Is my only concern paying child support, or do I love her so much that I don't want to lose her? I guess both might be true, but I want Lea.*

41

Love and lust, what's the difference? They both lead to sex. I got to have Lea."

He made his move. He gently slid out of the covers, but it was not gentle enough. Donna woke up. "Where are you going?"

"To the bathroom. I had more to drink than usual." The lie worked. She turned over and went back to sleep. Once in the bathroom, he looked into the mirror. *"What am I doing? I'm acting like a jealous boyfriend. This chick said it was a no strings attached deal. I can't catch feelings about this. Let me get my behind back in bed. I should have got some from my wife."* Jonathan returned to the bed and attempted to sleep.

The alarm went off. It was six and Jonathan rose to hit the gym. Donna asked, "Do you have to go, babe?"

"I need to stay in shape, baby. When we get back, I want to be ready for tri-outs."

"You'll make the team. You always do." She rolled over, "One morning can't hurt. Come here." She pulled him back into the bed. He hated how he felt. Donna was not the one he wanted. He couldn't understand the hold Lea had on him, but if he did not stay with Donna, she would ask questions. *"I guess I won't be getting any from Lea."*

The last day in Jamaica rolled by without event. Jonathan and Donna spent the day alone. They could not find Ray and Vanessa, but rationalized that they would see them at dinner in the main dining room.

Jonathan looked everywhere, hoping to catch a glimpse of Lea, but he did not. He enjoyed the time with Donna but could not get his mind off Lea. He sat on the bed waiting for Donna to finish dressing for dinner. The ship set sail an hour before. They would be back at the port the next morning, then back in Panama City that evening. He thought about his girls and smiled. *"I need to stop this lustful behavior, if for no other reason than them. Imagine what they would think of me if they grew up knowing their dad cheated on their mom. I'll do better. Once I'm off this ship, I won't see Lea again. I will do right from now on."*

Donna walked out of the bathroom, and Jonathan caught himself imagining her as Lea. He smiled, hoping it did not show on his face. Jonathan hopped up and hugged Donna, then gave her a big kiss. She asked, "To what do I owe this honor?"

"Hey, you're the best wife ever. I'm the luckiest man ever."

"You're right on both counts. Now let's go eat." They arrived at their assigned table. Donna continued, "Where's Ray and Vanessa? We haven't seen them all day and now they're not here."

"Maybe they're just late."

"Maybe, but I'm hungry."

"So am I. We haven't eaten since breakfast."

"I know. I hope there's something really good on the menu today."

Jonathan said, "Has there been anything bad so far? The food is great on this ship."

"You got that right, baby." She smiled, "Hey, there's my girl." Donna rose and hugged Vanessa. She asked, "Where's Ray?"

Vanessa looked at Jonathan and said, "You knew, didn't you?"

Jonathan answered, "Knew what?'

"Don't pretend Jonathan!"

Donna jumped in, "Hold it. Now if my husband did something, then let me handle it. What's going on here, Vanessa?"

"My husband cheated with that twin, Mia. I caught them together. When we get back, I'm divorcing him." She looked at Jonathan, "You knew, and you've been with the other one, haven't you?"

Donna interjected, "My husband has been with me the entire time. Now, I'm sorry for what you're going through. No one knows it better than me about cheating, but this time, he's innocent. Don't drag him down because you caught her husband."

Jonathan felt horrible inside, but he was glad Donna took up for him. If he had to speak, the truth might come out and that would not be good for his marriage.

Vanessa said, "One day, Donna, you'll learn the truth." She turned and walked away.

Donna sat back down, "Why is she so sure you cheated?"

"Don't ask me. Like you said, I was with you the whole time. You can't pin this on me. Come on, baby."

"I know. You're right. I feel bad for her, though."

Jonathan looked up, and Lea was with the same man. Anger welled up inside again. *"How could she do this to me?"* He tried not look, knowing his anger would show and he would need to explain it.

Donna said, "Well, there's the twin she thought you were with. It's clear she's got herself a man."

"I know, right. I don't know why she's trying to drag me down." *"I wonder did Ray, sell me out? He's the only one who knows about me and Lea."* Jonathan did not notice Ray's arrival at the table. Donna's look of shock alerted him that something was wrong. Jonathan said, "Ray, dude, you're here and with… Mia. Wow, dude, your wife was just here."

Ray said, "I know. I broke the news to her earlier. Me and Vanessa are getting a divorce, then I'm going to marry Mia."

Jonathan's jaw dropped. "Really? You guys just met."

"I know, man, but we're in love." Ray and Mia sat down at the table.

Donna jumped up, "I'm not staying for dinner."

Jonathan said, "But you're hungry. Where are you going?"

"I'm not taking part in this." She looked at Ray, "How could you do this to your wife? You're here on your anniversary and you leave her?" Mia snickered. Donna stepped toward her, "You think this is funny?"

Jonathan stepped between them. He had to get Donna out of there before his exploits became the topic of discussion. Jonathan said, "Wait, honey. You're right, let's get out of here." He turned to Ray, "Sorry, man, but we're leaving." Ray nodded, and Jonathan guided Donna out of the main dining area. He looked in Lea's direction and she was smiling at him. Lea waved seductively at him. Jonathan quickly returned his attention to Donna. He could not let on about Lea.

GERALD C. ANDERSON, SR.

Chapter 4

Jonathan waited for Donna by the car. As Vanessa cried, he watched. He suspected Vanessa was spilling her guts about Ray and Mia. He prayed his name would not be dragged into it. *"For once, I shouldn't be the topic of conversation. Lord knows I've hurt Donna enough. Now that Lea is behind me, I can do the right thing."*

Donna hugged Vanessa and headed toward Jonathan. Jonathan wanted to score some points, so he got out of the car and opened the door for his new bride. She smiled and kissed him. He got the points he wanted.

The drive back to Panama City was uneventful. They made small talk and Ray and Vanessa dominated the conversation. Donna expressed her anger at Ray's behavior and praised Jonathan. Jonathan kept his actions and emotions to himself. He thanked God he would never see Lea again. The temptation was too great for him to withstand. Now she would be a memory. Then there was Simone to deal with. He hoped she was still against him because he could not resist her if she wanted him.

They pulled up to the house where Donna's mother waited with the kids. Jonathan was glad to be home. After the wedding and honeymoon, he wanted to relax in their duplex, enjoy his girls, and write some music.

Donna opened the door, and Chloe and Zoe ran to them. The embrace was the greatest feeling Jonathan ever felt. He loved his girls.

After unpacking his suitcase and playing with his kids, Jonathan sat at his piano. He had a tune in his head he wanted to get down before he lost it. However, his mother-in-law had different plans. "Jonathan, you got a moment?"

"I wanted to get this tune down. Can it wait?" She rolled her eyes in that manner that reminded Jonathan that his mother-in-law was not one to play. "Okay, never mind. What's up, momma?"

"I know what happened on your wedding night and Donna told me everything about the cruise. Deep inside, she wonders if you cheated with that twin, but she believes you. I hope you didn't cheat on her again. That entire incident with Simone was enough for any woman to endure. Stop the cheating. You will never find true love by sleeping around."

"Momma, I have turned over a new leaf. I only went to that bar to tell Simone that I didn't want her coming around. My marriage is important to me, and I don't need her bothering me or Donna."

Ms. Williams lowered her head. She paused, then started, "That's a lie and we all know it. You went there to convince Simone to have sex with you. We know that for sure, and the sooner you admit it and ask for forgiveness, the better everyone will be."

"How can you be so sure?"

"You really got to ask that question?"

"I guess not. Look momma, I had those thoughts when I went down there, but I changed my mind. Simone thought that's what I wanted, but I didn't. I actually saved her from my boy Terrance, who would have dogged her. As for the twin, I didn't do anything with her. Ray was all into Mia, but I didn't want to cause any issues with my wife. Donna even said we were together all the time, so I couldn't have done anything."

"That's what she said, so it appears you're cleared of that one… maybe. Just keep it in your pants, son. My daughter loves you. I don't know why. She could do much better."

"Momma!"

"Donna, I'm just telling the truth. You shouldn't have to go through all of this with a man."

Jonathan was angry inside. His mother-in-law always talked badly about him, but what could he really say? He committed the offenses they accused of and a few more they did not know about. Jonathan said, "I think I'm going to bed. Good night, ladies." They each said good night and Jonathan left the room, hearing them argue. Donna was telling her mom politely to stay out of her marriage. He appreciated the support, but knew he did not deserve it.

Jonathan climbed in the bed and slowly fell off to sleep to the rhythm of Donna and her mom arguing loudly in the living room.

Monday morning fought its way into Jonathan's life. He woke and got dressed as usual. It was his job to take the girls to daycare while Donna would pick them up in the afternoon. The girls were up and having breakfast while Donna was heading out the door. She had to be at work at seven, while Jonathan had to be at work at 7:30. He kissed Donna bye, and she rushed out the door. Twenty minutes later Jonathan gathered the girls up and headed out himself.

The morning went by quick. Jonathan and Terrance hit the NCO Club for lunch. It was time to catch up on what was going on at the base while

Jonathan was away. He knew Simone returned to the base and worked her usual job at the Billeting office, but he wanted to know more. Jonathan wanted to know if she was back because of him and why was she really in New York when he was getting married? She was a great side piece, and he wanted another chance, but it had to be discreet. He could not let Donna know anything about it.

Jonathan arrived at the club. Terrance sat in their usual spot, waiting for him. "Hey, Jonathan. What took you so long?"

"The captain wanted me to finish up the punishment on an Article 15. Sorry, bro. What's been going on?" They exchanged their regular handshake and bro hug. "I'm so out of the loop?"

Terrance answered, "Nothing, dude. The same old things. I came here last night, but it was nothing happening. Your girl was here, though. She was hot as usual."

"Simone?"

"Yeah, man. She wore a blue dress that got everybody's attention, especially mine."

"Who hit on her?"

"Nobody. She was with Regine and some other girl. I got a dance with her, but she doesn't want any parts of me. Probably because of you."

"Probably."

"Anyway, how was the cruise?"

"Man, it was awesome. There were these twins on the ship… dude, you would have been all over them. I met up with this dude, Ray, and he went after one of them. Man, his wife caught him and now they're getting a divorce."

"You didn't go after the other one?" Jonathan snickered. "You did, didn't you? My boy, yeah. I take it Donna didn't catch you."

"No, man. My game is strong, but Ray's game was raggedy. He fell head over heels for that girl. You can't be catching feelings with your side pieces."

"I know that's right, dude. Are you going to see her again?"

"No, man. What happens on the ship stays on the ship. Besides, she's stationed in DC. I'm not going all the way up there for something I can get here. These Panama City girls will satisfy my side urges."

Terrance asked, "She's in the Air Force?"

"Yeah, a staff sergeant."

"Wow, at least she's not stationed here, but I thought you were going to be the good husband?"

"I thought about it so much, but I'm a young man and I can't leave all these women on the table. I love Donna and I can't stand to lose her, but I got to have what I need."

Terrance grinned, "Man, if I had your wife, I wouldn't cheat at all."

Jonathan grinned, "That's what every man says about another man's wife. I'll say it to you when you get married."

"When I get married, I will be retired from these streets. Your mistake was getting Donna pregnant. You should have worn a helmet."

"I think about that every day, but there's nothing I can do about it. For now, I'll try to be the good husband, but if Simone comes back, that's a wrap. I just have to make sure my game is tight, and she doesn't catch feelings again."

"You know she will."

"Yeah, well, I need to head back to work, man. I got so much to catch up on."

"Yeah, me too." The two men headed back to their respective workplaces. Throughout the day, Jonathan thought about Simone and Lea. Deep inside, he wanted to be the good husband, but his lustful urges were hard to resist. Having sex with Donna would never be enough for him. The excitement of getting with another woman on the side was too strong. *"It's a good thing Lea isn't here. I know I wouldn't be able to resist that."*

It was the end of the day, and Donna called Jonathan at work. "Hey, Donna. What's going on?"

"I need you to swing by the commissary and pick up some hamburger meat for dinner. I'll make your favorite spaghetti for us."

"With the sausage?"

"Yes, Jonathan." She laughed.

Jonathan enjoyed hearing her laugh. It made him feel good inside. "Okay, I can do that. Anything else you need, sweetheart?"

"Just my handsome husband."

"Oh baby, you got it. Hey, do we have any wine at home?"

"Probably not. You can pick that up, too."

"You got it, Donna. I can't wait to get home to you and my darling babies."

Donna laughed, "I can get used to this married thing. I know we've only been back one day, but I'm liking it a lot."

"Me too. I got to run, but I'll see you in a few."

"You got it, Jonathan."

Jonathan hung up the phone and smiled. *I really enjoy the married life. I just need to get rid of this lust inside of me. Why can't I resist other women, especially when I have such a good one at home? Maybe I should talk to Chaplain Henderson about it… nope, bad idea.*

Jonathan finished up his work and headed to the commissary. He grabbed the hamburger meat and a few other items. He headed to checkout but remembered he needed to grab some chips. Jonathan loved to snack on chips while he watched a good movie, something he knew they would do that evening.

He arrived at the chip aisle and searched for a bag he wanted, and that Donna would like. Behind him, a voice said, "Jonathan!" He turned and his eyes popped. "Well, isn't this a surprise? Jonathan Rose domesticated. I never thought I would see the day."

"Simone, so you're all signed into the base. How was your trip to New York?"

"My trip was good. I drove here and enjoyed the sights. Something I realized I need to do after my heartbreak."

Jonathon popped his lips. "I didn't really believe you were coming back here."

"I did my year in Korea and requested to return here. I live in Panama City. I didn't want you to run me away."

"I would never run you away, Simone."

"Please! You ran me away the moment you ditched me and went back to Donna."

"For the record, Simone, I never left Donna. You knew that and agreed to everything. You caught feelings and now you want to blame me."

"You know, Jonathan, you're right. It was my fault, but it will never happen again."

Jonathan asked, "Can I ask you a question?"

"Sure, for old times' sake."

"Why did you call Donna in the hotel and tell her I came down to talk to you?"

Simone laughed, "Me— call Donna? Jonathan, even you should know I would never call Donna and tell her anything."

"Well, if you didn't then—" Jonathan caught himself.

Simone finished his sentence, "Who did? There was only one other person in that bar. What can't you comprehend... that your boy would do that?"

"No, I can't. There had to be another person who saw me."

"Keep telling yourself that, but your boy was all over me, baby. He was angry when you interrupted him that time two years ago. I wouldn't have given him none. I don't do friends. I can't have all of you comparing notes about me like that."

"Simone, me and Terrance go back to basic training together. He would never betray me."

"I grow tired of this conversation. Have a good evening. Oh, and you know you're going to get the sour cream and onion chips. Donna loves those."

She walked away. Jonathan could not resist her sway. He shook his head and went back to selecting his chips. In his selection process, he could not stop thinking about Simone's words. He would never believe Terrance would turn on him, but if Simone did not call Donna, who did?

He grabbed the sour cream and onion chips, paid for his groceries, and headed to the Class VI store for the wine. In the Class VI store, he ran into Ed. "Hey it's my boy, Ed. What's up dude?"

"Hey, I heard you were back. How's married life?"

"Good. We've had some hiccups, but we're working it out."

"Terrance told me about Simone in the hotel bar. Dude, you got balls."

"I didn't do anything, man. We just talked about old times and why she was in New York." Ed smirked and nodded his head up and down. "I'm serious man, we only talked."

"Okay, I got you."

"Hey, just between me and you, do you think Terrance would call Donna and tell her about me and Simone in the bar?"

Ed laughed, "You've got to be kidding, right? Terrance? He'd never do that."

"That's what I thought, but I just talked to Simone, and she said she didn't make the call. Somebody called Donna, and I just assumed it was Simone. Now Simone is pointing the finger at Terrance."

Ed put his hand on Jonathan's shoulder, "She's lying. You know Simone is just trying to hurt you in any way she can. She made that call and now she wants you to think it was Terrance. We're solid as a rock and none of us would betray the other like that. You know it."

"I do, and I shouldn't have let her get to me. You're right Ed, she made that call."

"Absolutely. Now get your wine and go home to the wife and kids."

"I'm about to do that. Take care, brother."

"Hey, DJ Smooth Keys is at the club Wednesday. Let's hit it."

"Count me in… if I get a kitchen pass."

"Alright, Jonathan."

Jonathan grabbed their favorite wine and headed home. He could not wait to see his bride and his children. The ladies in his life made his day. He wanted to get rid of the thoughts of Simone and what she said. He wanted to focus on his family and enjoy the evening.

Chapter 5

It was Wednesday evening, and Jonathan convinced Donna to let him go to the club with Terrance and Ed. She threatened divorce if he cheated on her, but Jonathan was proud of himself. He resisted Simone and felt inside, if he could resist her, he could resist any woman.

Jonathan pulled up in the club parking lot. He arrived at ten, their customary time. He walked inside the club. Terrance and Ed garnered a table near the dance floor. Jonathan said, "Man, DJ Smooth is at it again! No one spins the music better than him."

Terrance said, "I know that's right, bro. I got you a beer, dude."

"Thanks, Terrance. Let's toast to good wives who grant kitchen passes to their husbands." The men drank their drinks and slammed the bottles on the table. Jonathan said, "Now, where's my prey?"

Jonathan spent the next few hours flirting and dancing with several women around the club. Ed asked, "Jonathan, are you selecting women you know would never sleep with you?"

The question shocked Jonathan, "Why do you ask that?"

"Because you typically go after women who don't know you. Easy targets. I've watched you for three years and I know your style. You select a new girl at the base, someone unsuspecting, and you treat her like a queen. Until you get what you want, then the real you come out." Ed laughed. "That chick over there would have been a prime Jonathan target. She just got here a couple of days ago, but you avoided her like the plague."

Jonathan stared at him. Inside, he knew Ed was right. He changed. There were several women in the club that made perfect targets, including the one Ed mentioned, but he went after the ones he knew he could not get. He looked down, "Maybe you're right, Ed. Maybe inside, I do want to retire from pimping."

Ed said, "There's no shame in leaving the game, man. You have a great wife. If… when I leave the game, I can only hope to have a wonderful queen at home waiting for me."

"Ed, I need to be honest with you. My wife, she's my life, man, but these urges I have inside.

Sometimes they're uncontrollable. I guess that's why I'm going after women who are impossible to get. I don't want to be successful because I know I can't fight the urge."

"Wow, that's deep, bro."

"Where's Terrance?"

"Said he was going to make a call. Some chick he's trying to get with. He wants her badly, but she wants nothing to do with him."

Jonathan looked in the corner of the club, and there was Simone. His nemesis. He was proud of his stance in the commissary, but what if she wanted him? What would he do then?

"Earth to Jonathan. Are you there, man?"

"There's Simone, sitting in the corner."

Ed turned and looked. He turned back, "Are you going to talk to her?"

"No, not this time. The last two conversations haven't gone well. I think that ship has sailed, man."

Ed nodded his head, "Probably for the better. That thing with her and Donna was scary. Frankly, I'm surprised Donna forgave you for it."

"You and me both. I think I'm going to head out, man. Tell Terrance I left."

"Will do, bro. How about we all do lunch tomorrow?"

"I'm taking the wife to lunch. How about Friday? We can hit that new Mexican joint outside the gate."

Ed smiled, "Sounds good. I'll tell Terrance."

Jonathan nodded and headed for the door. He looked at Simone and she smiled at him. He resisted the urge to go over to her and continued to his car. Behind him she said, "So, you can resist me now?"

Jonathan stopped and turned around, "Yeah, I can. You fell in love when you shouldn't have. You knew what we had, and you broke our deal. It almost cost me my future with my family."

"Your future is with me, Jonathan, whether you believe it or not." She turned and walked away, leaving Jonathan in the parking lot wondering what she meant. He had no intention of getting involved with her again. He admired his strength to stay away from her, but now she was coming after him. Would he need to tell Donna? He thought against doing that because it would start trouble where trouble did not need to exist.

Jonathan pulled up to his duplex. He came inside and Donna was sitting on the loveseat in the dark. She rolled her eyes at him, "Whoa, what are you doing sitting here in the dark?"

"Wondering why you're still messing with Simone? I told you I would divorce you."

"I didn't do anything with Simone, Donna. She came to the club late. I saw her as I was leaving. I walked out of the club and she came up behind me and asked me was I strong enough to resist her now. I told her yes. I swear, I did nothing."

"Liar. I'm filing in the morning." She got up and went to the bedroom in tears.

Jonathan followed behind her, "Donna, I swear I didn't do anything. Ask Ed. He'll tell you, I didn't do anything."

"You were flirting with every woman in the club then you and Simone left together."

"What? That's not what happened. Who's telling you this stuff?" Donna did not answer. Jonathan sighed. "Look baby, you don't think that I heard you tell me if I cheated, you would leave me? Why would I go to the club, where everyone on the base can see me and do exactly what you warned me not to do? I'm a married man now. I can't be out there like that. I'm innocent."

The phone rang, and Donna answered. She said a few words, but mostly listened to the person on the other end. Then she said, "Thanks Erica." She hung up the phone. "You've been somewhat cleared. Simone followed you outside and came back in after about five minutes, but you did flirt with women in the club."

"I didn't flirt with anyone. I asked them for dances and only to fast songs. I really didn't do anything this time."

"You've got a reprieve. Be happy. Good night, Jonathan." She got under the covers and turned away from Jonathan. One thing was for sure, there would be no intimacy that night.

The next morning, Jonathan dropped his girls off at daycare and rushed to his office. The first thing he did was call Simone. She answered, "Tyndall Air Force Base Lodging, Airman Wilson, may I help you?"

"Simone, I'm tired of you messing with me and my wife. Stop calling her and telling her these lies."

"I don't know what you're talking about, Jonathan, and I don't have time for this game."

"You know exactly what I'm talking about. As soon as I left the club, you called Donna and told her lies about me. You told her we left the club together when you know that's not true."

"Jonathan, I didn't call your wife. Goodbye." She hung up the phone, and that made Jonathan madder.

He spent the morning running the night through his head. Simone was the only one who could have made the call, and he knew it. What he did not know was why she did it.

Jonathan left his office and arrived at Donna's office. She worked in the records section of personnel. Soon as he pulled up, she jumped into the car and leaned over to kiss him. He hoped the kiss was a sign that she was not mad at him any longer.

The couple arrived at the NCO Club. Jonathan ordered for both of them. That was a trait that Donna adored in her man. Not only ordering for her, but knowing what she liked. She told Jonathan if a man can't order for his woman, then he has not taken the time to master her likes and dislikes. Jonathan did study Donna and study what she liked and disliked. He picked up that trait from one of his boys growing up to study women, determine what they like, and give it to them. This lesson got him in bed with a lot of women and got him Donna's heart.

The couple made small talk while they waited for their food. Erica walked into the club and joined them at the table. She said, "Hey, guys. Isn't this so sweet. You guys having lunch together."

Jonathan replied, "No thanks to people like you."

"What's that supposed to mean?"

"I'm tired of you and others like you calling my wife and lying on me. I was not flirting with anyone last night."

Erica's face tightened, "Yes, you did. You didn't leave with Simone but, oh yes, you were flirting with others. I told Donna, there's nothing wrong with a little flirting in the club. What matters is that you don't' take it home."

Donna added, "Look, now is not the time to discuss this. Me and my husband have talked this out and we're good. So let's forget it." Jonathan and Erica did not respond. Donna continued, "So, Erica, how was the club last night?"

"Good, except for Ed chasing after me. Why on Earth would your friend think I'd want to be with him, Jonathan?"

"Ed's a good brother. You would do well with him."

Erica and Donna laughed. Erica said, "You're joking, right?"

"No, I'm not joking. Of the three of us, Ed is probably the best of us. He's kindhearted and can be trusted. I'm rehabilitating under the counseling of my beautiful wife." Donna smiled. "One day, I'll be as good as Ed, so you would do well to date him."

Erica twisted her head, "Not going to happen. Everyone knows the three of you are dogs."

"Not me anymore." The food arrived, and Jonathan was glad for the distraction. He asked Erica, "Are you ordering?"

"No." She looked at Donna, "So, I will call you tonight. Is that good?"

Donna replied, "Yeah, girl. Are you sure you're okay?"

"Yeah, I'm fine. I'll call you." She got up and left the table.

Donna said, "I know my girl, and something is bothering her."

"I'm sure you'll find out tonight. How's your sandwich?"

"Good, and how's your sandwich?"

"It's good." They made small talk while eating. Jonathan enjoyed the rest of his lunch hour. After dropping Donna off at work, he returned to his office. He walked into the legal office and Simone was standing at the reception desk. He frowned at her, and she returned the stare. Jonathan pondered if he should say something to her, but choose not to. He walked to his office, hoping she would not follow him.

His hope was wrong; she followed him. "What do you want, Simone?"

"The lady at the front desk asked if you would do my power of attorney." He looked her in the eyes, wondering if she was telling the truth. Simone continued, "You can call her if you like. I have no desire to be here either, but I need this for my mom."

Jonathan decided it would be easier to just do it and get it out of the way. "Let me see your worksheet." Simone handed him the worksheet and her legal assistance card. He filled out the card, then prepared her power of attorney. They sat quietly while he worked, something he was thankful for. When he finished, Simone was smiling at him. "Why are you smiling at me like that?"

"There was a time when we would have talked the entire time, but now we have nothing to say to each other. It's just funny how things change."

"Yeah, isn't that funny? If you weren't so vindictive, maybe we could have been friends."

"Dude, I really don't know what you're talking about. I haven't talked to Donna since I left for Korea."

"Here's your power of attorney. Read it over, then we can notarize it for you."

Simone read over the document, "Looks good to me."

"Okay, I need your ID card." She handed him the card, and she signed the document. Jonathan notarized it. "Here you go."

"Thank you, Jonathan, and with all seriousness, I haven't told Donna anything. I hope you figure it out." She walked out of his office. Inside, he was believing her. If she was telling Donna lies about him, she would take responsibility for it.

The end of the day came quick for Jonathan. He headed home to be with his family, but expected more lies to be waiting for him. He dropped by the grocery store and picked up some fresh roses for Donna, hoping to stem the anger a bit. *"Simone was in my office, so she probably called Donna and told her some more mess. These should help ease her anger. After all, I know my wife and she loves flowers."*

Jonathan arrived home to a bustling house. Donna was busy with dinner and the girls came running to their dad. Jonathan said, "This never gets old." Both girls hugged him tightly. Jonathan made his way over to Donna and gave her a hug and a kiss.

She said, "Are those for me?" Donna smiled and took the flowers from Jonathan.

"Of course they are for you. There's no other deserving woman in the universe."

"Aww, you're so sweet, baby. Go get cleaned up. Dinner will be ready in a few."

"Awesome." He walked to the bedroom, answering questions from his two daughters. They wanted to come into the bedroom with him, but he explained they could not since he had to change clothes. Jonathan assured them he would come back and play with them. *"I love those two more than anyone could ever know."*

Jonathan changed his clothes and returned to the living room. The girls waited for him to make good on his promise, and he did. They laid on the floor coloring in their coloring books while Donna finished making dinner. Jonathan thanked God for allowing his home to be peaceful. He wondered if Simone was right, and she did not feed Donna any information. Telling her she was in the legal office and being helped by Jonathan would have been something she would not resist. So if it was not Simone, who was it? That was a question that would need to be answered another day. Today, he would enjoy his family.

Later that evening, once the kids were asleep, Jonathan and Donna watched a movie while sipping on their wine. Jonathan looked on and off at his wife and was proud. These moments he cherished. She asked, "Jonathan, why do men cheat?"

The question struck him like a gut punch. He thought his peaceful evening was at an end. He questioned why she waited all evening to interrogate him about Simone. "For me, it was a matter of upbringing. There was no real father figure in my life, so everything I learned about women came from the streets. In the streets we're judged by the number of notches on our bedpost. That's what makes us men."

She replied, "That's such nonsense. What makes you a man is how you treat your woman and your children. Any fool can make a baby, but a man takes care of his responsibility."

"Hey, don't shoot the messenger." He wanted to deflect the conversation from him. Jonathan and his buddies lived by a code of manhood. To them, if you're only with one woman, you're not a man. He continued, "Baby, I learned my lesson. You're right, being a man is not how many women you sleep with but how you care for your one woman and the children you make." He laughed inside, knowing he did not believe a word of that.

Donna said, "I really hope you've changed, Jonathan. It's evenings like this that make life worthwhile. I want my marriage to be filled with these types of days. Not with me sitting at home wondering if you're sleeping around."

"Baby, I gave that up." He smiled a reassuring smile to her. *"There's no way I'm really going to do this. If someone comes along, all bets might be off… but in the meantime, this is good, too."*

The blaring sound of the alarm filled the Rose bedroom. Jonathan reached over and shut it off. It was time for another day to begin. At least it was Friday, and it would go by fast. That's what Jonathan hoped.

The couple dressed. Donna got the kids ready and handed them off to Jonathan. She kissed him and rushed out of the house, not wanting to be late for work. Jonathan asked the kids, "You guys ready for school?" They both shouted 'yes'. Jonathan wondered where they got the energy.

In the car, Jonathan's cell rang. "Hey, boy, what's up?"

Ed replied, "Dude, remember that new girl I told you about in Supply Squadron?"

"Yeah, you hit that?"

"No, but she asked about you?"

"Me? I don't know any new girl."

"But you do. Her name is Lea."

Jonathan laughed, "Stop lying, dude. You almost had me."

"I'm not lying, dude. I met her at the Rec Center last night and she asked if you were still stationed here."

"What did you tell her?"

"I told her yeah and that you would be at the club for happy hour tonight."

"No you didn't!"

"Yes, I did."

Jonathan popped his lips, "Dude, if that's the same Lea, you know I can't resist her. I want to be the good husband."

"Jonathan, brother, you can do this on the down-low, man. Remember, me and Terrance got you covered."

Jonathan gave it some thought. If Lea was stationed on Tyndall, it would be great. She could handle an affair and not catch feelings, but he would need to guard his feelings. She had him strung out after one time on the ship. He couldn't imagine what she would do now. He said, "I can't believe you set this up, man. Now you need to make sure Donna doesn't find out about this. Someone is leaking her information. I don't know who it is, so I don't know how to avoid them."

"She won't tell you?"

"No, she won't. She probably won't tell me because she doesn't want me avoiding them."

"Makes sense. Trust me, I got you and you know Terrance has you. You won't get caught."

"Alright, dude. I'll be there."

"Good. See you later, bruh."

"Later." Jonathan hung up the phone and took the kids into the Daycare Center. Once they were in their class, Jonathan headed for work. He could not get Lea off his mind. *"All I asked for was a chance to be the good husband and now temptation is smacking me in the face. I want to resist; I need to resist… I can't resist. I need to have it one more time."*

Chapter 6

The end of the day came fast for Jonathan...
too fast. Part of him wanted to hit the club and meet up
with Lea, but another part wanted to be faithful to
Donna. He struggled with his decision all day, but
fortunately for him, Chloe bailed him out. His desk
phone rang, and he answered, "Military Justice Sergeant
Rose, may I help you?"

"Hi this is Lauren Dixon from the Daycare
Center."

"Hi Ms. Dixon."

"Hi, Chloe is sick. Can you pick her up early?
She may need to go to the clinic."

Inside, Jonathan was happy. They bailed him
out. "I'll be right over to pick her up."

"Thank you, Sergeant Rose."

"Thank you." He hung up the phone, *"Thank you Chloe!"* Jonathan rushed to the Daycare Center. Chole was lethargic. He picked Zoe up as well and took both girl's home. On his way home, he called Donna, "Hey babe, I had to pick the girls up. Chloe isn't feeling well."

"Okay, there's a virus going around the center. I'll bring some stuff home for her."

"Thanks." He hung up the phone and called Ed. "Hey bruh, I can't make the club. My daughter is sick. I had to pick her up from daycare."

"Oh man, you're going to miss out. You know that honey has options."

"Hey, my daughter comes first, man. What can I say?"

"I hear you dude. That's why I'm still single with no kids."

Jonathan smiled, "Yes, that is why, but I wouldn't trade my girls for nothing in the world."

"I know you wouldn't. I'll fill you in later."

"Bet." He hung up smiling that fate gave him a break, and he did not have to make the choice. He could not resist the thoughts of Lea in his head. The morning he spent with her on the ship was the best he had, and he wanted more, but the price would be high. He had Donna's trust, but his leash was not long.

Jonathan arrived home and got the girls into the house. Chloe laid in Jonathan's bed while Zoe played on the bedroom floor. Jonathan laid next to his sick daughter. They loved being under their mom when they were sick, but Jonathan caressed them when he had the opportunity. He heard the front door and Zoe ran up front to greet Donna.

Jonathan heard Donna and Zoe exchange I love you gestures, then she headed back to him. Even after a long day in uniform, she was still beautiful to him. Donna asked, "How is she?"

"The same." He stood and embraced his wife. She hugged him back and kissed him. It was not the usual welcome home kiss. Jonathan asked, "Are you okay?"

"Yeah, I'm just tired and you know I get worried when one of my babies isn't feeling well."

"I know. Well, she's been resting since we got home. I gave her some Pedialyte for the diarrhea and children's Tylenol. Since we've been home, she's been sleeping."

"Okay, can we order pizza today? I don't feel like cooking."

"We sure can. The usual?"

"Yes." She turned to walk out, but stopped. She looked at him. Jonathan nodded his head, trying to determine what she was thinking. She continued, "I heard the other twin is stationed here now, and you were going to meet her at the club."

"What? Ed asked me to go to the club this morning. I never agreed to go and what twin?"

"You know dang well what twin?"

"From the ship? I told you nothing happened on the ship. Wow, I can't believe you're bringing this to me now. Okay, I haven't been the best boyfriend or husband, but can't I get a break? If I wanted to meet someone at the club, I would have told you to get the girls. You're the one who picks them up every day, anyway."

Donna appeared to think about his words. He made a great argument, and he was glad he was a father first. If he had gone to the club, he would have been in big trouble. She replied, "Okay, again, you seem to be innocent."

"Who is telling you these things?"

"It doesn't matter." She walked out of the bedroom to the bathroom. Jonathan was furious. He did not know who was telling Donna, but he realized only two people knew about the meeting. He and Ed. Maybe Ed was calling his wife. He checked her cell records to see if she received a call from him. That would explain how she knew so many things.

He called Ed's cell phone. "Hey Ed."

"Hey buddy, are you on the way?"

"No, I'm not on the way. Did you tell Donna I was going to the club to meet up with Lea?"

"No man, I wouldn't do that."

"She knew about it and expected me to be there. She was going to catch me. Good thing Chloe got sick." The line was quiet. "If you didn't tell, who did?"

"I don't know, man, but I told Terrance and a couple of other people to be here, too. I thought if there was a group of us and Donna walked in she wouldn't suspect anything. Any of them could have told her. But hey, I will ask around and find out, man."

"Do that."

Ed sighed into the phone, "Dude, I'm your boy, and you know I would not betray you like that."

"Yeah, sorry, I lost my head. Find out for me."

"I will man."

Jonathan hung up the phone. He rubbed Chloe's head. She was still hot. Donna walked in with the thermometer and took her temperature. She said, "She still has a fever."

Jonathan said, "Maybe we should take her to the doctor."

"We'll give it some more time. Has Zoe acted sick?"

"No, she's been jumping around and having a good time."

"Okay, I'll order the pizza."

Jonathan replied, "No, I'll do it. You sit down and relax."

She looked at him. "I really hope you're not trying to be with someone else."

"Donna, please, let it go. I've proven to you twice now that I'm not doing that." He hit the wall with a soft fist. "Someone is trying to set me up." Donna starred at him. "You know who it is, so you should tell me who's feeding you this information."

"I will handle it because you're right. Twice now I've been told something that's turned out false. I will not listen to someone who's lying to me and ruining my marriage."

Jonathan truly had Donna's trust. The question is, will he abuse that trust? "I hope you do because if this keeps happening, I'm going to do something about it." Jonathan walked out of the room, hoping to have left an impression. Zoe tagged along behind him. Following his every move. "What are you doing, little girl?"

Zoe said, "I don't know, daddy."

He laughed and ordered the pizza. While waiting for the person to take his order, he watched his daughter playing on the floor. The side of him that wanted to be the good husband continued to struggle with the lustful side of him. He wondered what was going on at the club. Was Lea truly there and was she truly assigned to Tyndall? He had to find out, but he had to move in a way that no one would know. The person came on the line and took his order. He spent the rest of the evening relaxing and caring for his daughter.

Saturday morning came and brought with it an overcast day. The rain pounded on the windows. The thunder and lightning scared Zoe. She came running into her parent's room afraid of the sound. Jonathan grabbed Zoe and held her next to him. "It's okay, sweetheart. You're safe with daddy." He looked over at Donna, who was caring for Chloe, "I guess there goes the gym."

"You don't need to go anyway, since Chloe is sick. I need your help here."

Jonathan sat up, "You're right." He looked at his phone. Ed sent him a text, "Yo J, I think I know who's been diming you out. It might be DeAndre. He's been hitting on your wife."

Jonathan texted back, "Is that right? She never mentioned it."

"Yeah bro, you need to check him."

"I will." Jonathan locked his phone and looked over at Donna. He wanted to find out more about DeAndre hitting on her. *All this time, they have been focused on my infidelity and she's been talking to another man. Isn't that the pot calling the kettle black?* Jonathan stood up,

"So we're just going to sit at home all day? Maybe I should get us a movie or something?"

"Get a couple of movies. One for Zoe, and then one for us later."

"Sounds good. Do we need some wine too? I mean for later?"

"Yeah, I think we drank the last of it already. Can you go to the commissary and pick up some stuff to cook? We can't eat pizza every day."

"Sure, write a list for me. You know I'll forget stuff and bring back junk."

Donna snickered, "I know you will." She wrote the list out and handed it to Jonathan. He now had a reason to be on base. He could find out some information about DeAndre while he was there. Maybe see what was up with Lea if he had a chance. Donna asked, "I don't have to worry, do I?"

Jonathan sighed. He wanted to ask about DeAndre, but he needed his ducks in a row first. "No, and I wish you would stop that."

"I'm trying."

Jonathan nodded and walked out of the house. On the drive to the base, Jonathan called Terrance. "Hey man, I'm on my way to the base. Where does this DeAndre dude live?"

"He lives off base. He has a townhouse with his boy, Nate. They work in the Controller Squadron. Why you ask?"

"Dang, I was hoping to chat with him. Ed said he's been hitting on Donna."

"DeAndre? I don't think that's true."

"Really?"

"Yeah man, he won't tell you he's putting the moves on your wife. Besides, I think he's got someone."

Jonathan sighed, "When does that matter?"

"You right, but I know Donna isn't having it, man. She's not cheating on you."

"Yeah, but she's talking to him. Getting information from him. What she doesn't understand is this dude will tell her anything to get with her."

"That could be true. She should be careful. Are you going to confront her?"

"At some point."

"Cool. Are we still coming over tonight?"

"Coming over? Oh man, I forgot. Chloe is sick. Let me check with Donna and get back to you."

"Yeah soon man. I got this honey lined up to come with me."

"Alright, I'll hit you back in a minute." Jonathan hung up the phone and called Donna. She wasn't thrilled about Terrence and Ed coming over, but she agreed. She also insisted Erica and Rene come with their boyfriends. Jonathan gave into the request. He knew Donna hated having a couple's night with Terrence and Ed. It was mostly because they never brought the same woman twice. She liked consistently, and she hated both of them because of their ways.

Jonathan called Terrence back, and they agreed on the time for the meet. Jonathan arrived at the commissary and picked up the items Donna wanted. He checked out and returned to his car. He put the items in the trunk and closed it. When he closed the trunk, Lea was standing there. He was shocked but gathered himself quickly, "I heard you were stationed here. Funny, I didn't even know you were in the military."

"The topic never came up on the ship, did it? I mean, both our minds were somewhere else."

"No, it did not. What do we do now?"

She moved closer to Jonathan, "I was hoping we could pick up where we left off. We never really got the chance to continue." Jonathan felt himself sweating. He wanted her, but he was afraid for the first time to pay the price. She continued, "I know you're not scared. On the ship, you didn't seem scared to me."

His manhood felt challenged. "I'm not scared at all."

"Then let's get together."

"Okay, I can meet you tomorrow morning. I'll tell my wife I'm going to the gym."

She laughed, "Same as the ship."

"Hey, I'm an early gym rat."

"I see. I live in the Supply Squadron dorm, room 215. I don't have a roommate."

"Good, I'll see you there."

"I'll be waiting."

Jonathan asked, "Who was the guy you were with on the ship?" Lea laughed and walked away. Jonathan shook his head in disgust. He did not know if he was mad because she was with someone else or because she was just like him. He jogged to her car window. "Hey, did you tell anyone about us?"

Lea answered, "That's the quickest way to get busted so that would be a 'no'."

Jonathan nodded, "Good, because someone is telling my wife things and I'm not sure who it is right now."

"That could be dangerous."

"Yes, it could."

Lea said, "I hope you don't tell anyone."

"I'm not telling anyone right now. I'm not sure I can trust my two best friends at this point."

She smiled, "Dude, I don't tell my twin everything I do. You can't put your moves out to the public. That's how you get busted. If I find out you are talking, I'm out."

"I won't."

"Good." She shifted gears and drove away without waiting for a response. Her tall slender body captivated Jonathan. *"She had to be sculpted by God Himself. There's nothing on Earth better than her."*

Jonathan returned home and he and Donna prepared for the evening's festivities. Chloe felt better, and the kids would be in the bedroom. Donna's supervisor, Sergeant Sheppard, had a teenage daughter who watched the kids when Jonathan and Donna had plans.

Chapter 7

Rene and her husband and Ed and his date could not attend, so Jonathan, Donna, Terrance, his date and Erica and her date were gathered in Jonathan's living room. Jonathan couldn't get his mind off Lea. He wanted to tell Terrance, but that feeling of distrust surrounded his being. He watched his boy interact at the party, checking out his date, LaWanda. LaWanda was a pretty woman, with Indian features. She was tall and her skin color was a soft brown. Jonathan loved the look of her skin. She was one of the best looking women on Tyndall Air Force Base. Jonathan asked, "So, LaWanda, where did you come from?"

"Japan. I was stationed at Yokota for three years. I extended a year because I loved it there."

"Cool. Where do you work?"

Terrance chimed in, "What's with the 20 questions, man?"

"Making conversation. You don't want us to know who she is."

LaWanda said, "I can speak for myself." She popped her lips as if annoyed by Terrance, "I work in Cybersecurity."

Jonathan said, "Oh, that secured building."

"Yeah, we can't have everyone in our building. You need a top secret clearance to be in there."

"Interesting. I work in legal, and my beautiful wife works in personnel."

"Yeah, I met Donna last week. I had to check out my records."

Donna smiled while sipping on her drink. Jonathan watched her, hoping for a tell, "My wife is the best one to talk to over there. She's so smart."

"Okay, husband, what do you want?" Everyone burst out in laughter. "You know I know my husband. Compliments like that come with a price tag."

Jonathan laughed, knowing she was right. He wanted everything to be cool so he could slip off to the gym in the morning. Anger welled up inside when he noticed Donna and Terrance's eyes locked in on each other. He looked at each of them and recognized that look like nobody else. It was that look of hiding something. Jonathan wanted to smash Terrance in the face, but held his anger.

LaWanda said, "Donna, where are you from?"

"Right up the road, Montgomery. I joined the Air Force to see the world, girl."

They laughed and LaWanda replied, "I'm from Dallas. I wanted my first assignment to be overseas. I put everything overseas, hoping and praying I got it. When they told me I was going to Japan, I was happy, especially considering what happened at MEPS when I was coming into the Air Force."

Erica asked, "What happened?"

"Girl, you know how they bring you to MEPs for all the final paperwork before you go to basic. Well, some guy was hyped up on something and he raped a girl. He destroyed everything in that room. The police came and arrested him. I called my mom and told her to come get me. She didn't. She calmed me down and I went off to basic, but I wanted out of this country."

Donna said, "Wow, that's some story. For me, I wanted to be close to home. I wanted Maxwell, but they gave me Tyndall. I'm okay since I met my husband here."

Terrance said, "Yeah, aren't you the lucky one?"

Jonathan was furious, "What does that mean? What are you saying, dude?"

"Nothing, man. Your wife is lucky to have you. What's your problem?"

Donna said, "Jonathan, can you get me some more wine?"

Jonathan looked at her and rolled his eyes. She leaned her head to the side to insist she meant it. He went to the kitchen and grabbed the bottle of wine. He turned to bring it back and noticed the same look on Donna and Terrance's face. When he turned, Terrance quickly looked away from Donna, but Donna rolled her eyes at him more. Something was going on and Jonathan got angrier with each passing moment. Jonathan reached out his hand for Donna's glass and poured her wine. He handed it back to her. Inside, he wanted to pour the bottle on his friend. He wasn't sure if they were sleeping together or not, but something was going on.

The night rolled on, and Jonathan continued to watch Donna and Terrance. He tried not to be noticeable, but he decided he was going to be with Lea. He hated the fact that his wife was cheating on him and with his best friend. Jonathan decided he would punish them both. His dream would be to sleep with LaWanda, but he wasn't sure she liked Terrance.

Jonathan and Donna stood outside while the two couples were leaving. LaWanda said sternly to Terrance, "You can't even open my door? What kind of gentlemen are you?"

Jonathan smiled, thinking, *"This is the man my wife is sleeping with over me. At least I open her door all the time."*

The couples drove off. Jonathan looked Donna in the eye and sneered. Hate grew inside him. They walked inside and Donna took the babysitter home. Jonathan kissed his daughters on the forehead. His cell rang. It was Ed. "Hey brother, what's up?"

"How did the evening go?"

"It was revealing. What are you doing calling me? I thought you had a hot date."

"Yeah, not so hot. Apparently, this chick is known for sleeping around. I didn't want to catch anything."

"Yeah, that would not be good. I think my wife and Terrance and doing something."

Ed burst out in uncontrollable laughter. "You got jokes, brother."

"I'm not joking. I noticed them make eye contact all night. The contact I used to make when I had a honey in the room. If Terrance wasn't taking his date home, I believe they would be together now."

"Dude, your wife would never sleep with Terrance."

"So you and I believe. Maybe that's the cover."

"Look man, if Donna wanted revenge for your actions, she would tell you what she's doing, not keep it a secret. How is it revenge if you don't know?'

"You got a point, but something is going on. I can't put my finger on it."

Ed sighed, "Dude, you, Terrance, and I have been boys for a few years. You can't believe that he would sleep with your wife. Not to mention your wife doesn't play man. She would never be with Terrance."

"I don't know man. Something was up. My sense of loyalty to her is all but gone now. Terrance had a pretty girl over here tonight. Oh, man, she was hot."

"LaWanda?"

"Yeah, you saw her before?"

"Bruh, I did. She is fine and so pretty. Remember, though Terrance saw Simone first, and you took her. He hasn't…"

"That's right! Dude, I bet this is about Simone. He's trying to get me back by sleeping with my wife."

"Come on man, I'm sorry I brought it up. Remember, we are talking about Donna, not Simone."

"She's coming through the door; I'll talk to you tomorrow."

"Peace out, brother."

Jonathan hung up the phone. Donna joined him in the bedroom. She asked, "Any issues with the kids?"

"Nope, they are sleeping quietly."

"Who were you talking to?"

"Ed. Apparently, his date didn't go too well. The girl sleeps around with everyone in Panama City."

"Then that should have been right up Ed's alley."

Jonathan looked at her with disdain. "I can't believe you said that."

"So, it's bad when a woman sleeps around, but it's cool when you do it."

"Here we go again. I've been faithful to you."

"Not all the time."

"Since we had the discussion on the ship, I have been faithful to you. I can't change the past."

"Right, but Ed is still out there chasing different women and sleeping with more than one. He's got the nerve to condemn this girl when he does the same thing."

"Okay, let's talk about something else."

"Like?"

"Like the looks you and Terrence were sharing tonight. What's that all about?"

Donna rolled her eyes at him. He could not tell if she was angry because he busted her or if she thought he had the nerve for asking. "Are you seriously about to ask me if I'm sleeping with your best friend? The guy who I think is a jerk among all jerks? Are you about to ask me that?"

He thought twice about bringing the issue up without proof. She was getting mad with each passing second. He was about to spend the night on the couch. "Something is going on between the two of you."

Donna grabbed her night clothes. "I'll sleep with the girls tonight."

He dropped his head. *"That didn't go well, but hey, I'm getting laid in the morning, anyway. C'vest la vie."*

Jonathan could not sleep that night. He anticipated a great morning with Lea. He got up and changed into his gym clothes. It was nearing 8:00. Donna was still asleep in the girl's bedroom. He left a note for her on the coffee table and headed out the door.

There was little traffic on the road. Sunday mornings found most people asleep or in church. For Jonathan, it was easier to get to the base and perform his morning workout. Something he needed to do since basketball season was approaching. He needed to be on his game. Today would be a different workout, one he anticipated all night. He arrived at his job and parked near the building. The office was close to Supply's dorm. He would use work as his cover in case anyone noticed, and he needed an excuse. The excitement of having a sidepiece again welled up inside of him. He wondered if he was finding fault with Donna and Terrance, to explain away his lustful desires.

He arrived at the dorm and knocked on Lea's door. He hoped she would answer quickly since her door faced the street-side and someone could see him going into her room. She opened the door, and he went inside.

Her room was not what he expected. Donna was a neat freak, and everything in the house had its place. Lea's room was not like that. Clothes were thrown over chairs and shoes were all around the floor. He did not mind or care; he was there for one thing and one thing only.

Lea moved into his arms. She snuggled up to him. Her head laid in his chest. She was just the right height. He embraced her tightly into his physical being. Jonathan laid his head on top of hers and took in the aroma of her being. She smelled better than most women he had been with. Definitely better than the way she kept house. It was noticeable that she took care down to the smallest detail of her body. He knew she cared about the body she presented to him. For a moment, he thought about leaving and staying true to his word with Donna, but he allowed the thoughts of Donna and Terrance to continue to anger him.

She eased him toward the bed in a dancing motion. The closer she got to the bed, the more he rose in excitement. He wanted her more than ever. Once at the bed, he guided her down with no resistance. Jonathan eased the little clothing she wore off and kissed her, starting with the lips, then making his way down. He felt the explosion as her body tensed up with passion. He crossed the line again and enjoyed every moment of the experience.

For two hours, the pulsating vibe of lust abounded in Lea's dorm room. They kept their emotions silent for fear of being heard by others. When it was over, Jonathan laid back in her bed and relished the experience. He loved it. Jonathan thought, *"If I get a divorce over this, then so be it. She is the best I have ever had in my life."*

He looked over at Lea as she quietly slept. His manhood felt good that she fell asleep so fast. He hated to wake her, but he needed to leave. Two hours at the gym would be explainable, but any more than that, he would have issues. Jonathan slid out of bed and got dressed. Lea asked, "Is it time already?"

"Honey, it's been two hours."

"Hmm, that was fast. When will I see you again?"

"I'm not sure. I'll have to see what's going on at home."

Lea sat up, "Why don't you divorce her and be with me?"

The question stunned Jonathan. Was she catching feelings? He could not believe it. She preached so much about that very topic. He asked, "Why do you ask that? You aren't getting feelings for me, right?"

Lea sat up, "She doesn't make you happy. Your children make you happy and that's why you stay. Don't you want to be with someone you love?"

"I do love Donna."

Lea laughed, "After what you put on me, there's no way you love her. I'll call you at work tomorrow." She walked into the bathroom and Jonathan seized that moment to head out.

He walked out the door, down the stairs, and to his car. Simone's car pulled in front of him. She rolled down her window and asked, "So, are we up to our old games again? Who is it this time?"

"Leave me alone, Simone."

"Let me guess. You told Donna you were at the gym. The same lie you told her when you came to see me. A dog never changes his bark." She shook her head and drove off.

Jonathan figured it would not be long before Donna knew about this. He would have to get Ed to cover for him. He called him on his cell. "Ed, man, I need your help."

"What you need, bro?"

"I need you to say we were at the gym."

"I am at the gym. I'm just leaving now."

"Good, say I was with you. Simone saw me coming from the Supply dorm. I know she'll tell Donna."

"The Supply dorm? Let me guess, you hit Lea, right?"

"You know it, boy!"

"Don't worry, bro, I got you."

"Thanks, Ed. I can always count on you."

"You can count on Terrance too, man."

"Yeah, that's yet to be determined. I used to believe it, but now I'm not so sure. Anyway, I'm headed home. I'm sure Simone has called her by now."

"Alright, bro; be easy."

"You too." Jonathan hung up the phone and thought about his story. He knew Donna would be mad and ask him a ton of questions. He needed to stay cool and stick to the gym story. Everything would work out. He pondered Lea's question of why stay married to Donna. Why did he marry her? He thought the answer was clear, that he loved her, but the truth was he loved the kids. His problem was lust. He could not get enough of other women. Jonathan lived for the excitement of infidelity, the allure of another woman, the sneaking around. It all turned him on.

The thought of Lea catching feelings worried him. He did not need her to make trouble for him. The benefit of both of them being subject to the Uniform Code of Military Justice gave him some solace. If she told on him, she would go down too. He loved the sex and if he were single, he would date her, but he did not want to lose his family for her.

He pulled up in the driveway. Erica's car was parked in front of the house. *"Now, I'll have to deal with two of them. That's just great."* He walked into the house. Chloe and Zoe ran up to him and grabbed him. "Chloe, sweetheart, you're feeling better."

Donna said, "She woke up without a fever and has been running around since. I think it's past her now."

"Good. Hi, Erica."

"Hey, Jonathan."

Jonathan went to the bedroom, and the girls followed him. He said, "Come on guys, you know daddy has to shower and change. Soon as I'm done, we can play, okay?" They both said okay, and Jonathan showered and change. He hoped Erica's presence would delay the accusations made by Simone. Jonathan heard Erica making a point to Donna, but he could not make out the words. He wondered if she was telling Donna if she was wrong about her infidelity. The voices lowered and he could not hear anything. Jonathan stepped into the shower and washed the aroma that was Lea off his body.

Later that evening, Jonathan sat with the girls. He was reading them a bedtime story. The girls loved his antics when he read the stories, and Jonathan lived for it. It was a talent for him. Donna stood at the door. After he finished, she said, "You know you may have your shortcomings in loyalty, but you have a talent for reading stories to children."

GERALD C. ANDERSON, SR.

"I am loyal, but yes, I love reading these stories to my children. I promised myself I would be the world's best father. If nothing else, I will have that." Jonathan pushed past Donna and went into the kitchen. He said, "You're still here?"

Erica replied, "Someone needed to keep Donna company."

"What does that mean? I always keep her company."

"Yeah, when you're not in the streets chasing some woman."

Jonathan was offended, "You don't know what you're talking about. I'm committed to this marriage."

Donna walked in the room, "Erica, I thought we talked."

"We did, but I couldn't resist."

Jonathan said, "If anyone in this house has got a secret, it's Donna."

"What the Hell are you talking about? I don't have any secrets."

Jonathan did not want it to come out this way, but now that he said it, he would follow up on what he knew about Donna and Terrance. "I saw the way you and Terrence looked at each other last night. I'm not a fool, Donna. The two of you have something going on."

Erica laughed. Donna replied, "Not this again. You must be out of your mind. You truly think I would sleep with Terrance? Please."

"I saw the looks you two were giving each other."

Donna said, "Erica, he brought this crap up to me last night after you left. Can you believe he said this to me?"

Erica replied, "Donna, you might as well tell it all now, sister. I would love to see how this turns out, but I have a date with my boyfriend. He doesn't cheat."

Jonathan frowned at her. Inside, he could not stand Erica. She always called him out for his infidelity. Erica left the house and Jonathan shouted, "Why? Why Terrance, of all people?"

Donna laughed, "I told you before, I would never sleep with Terrance. But I told you if you slept with someone else again, I would divorce you."

"I've heard that already."

"I'm divorcing you tomorrow. I want you to call the First Sergeant and get a room in the dorm and be out of here by the end of the week." She did not wait for a response. Instead, she turned and headed to the bedroom.

Jonathan was angry. "Who are you to tell me to get out, and for no reason at that?"

"I know you were not at the gym this morning. You went to the Supply dorm and slept with someone. I don't know who, but when I do, I'll make both of you pay."

"You don't know what you're talking about, and you certainly shouldn't take Simone's word for it."

Donna turned and rolled her eyes at him, "So, Simone has something to do with this?"

Jonathan did not know how to respond. He gave up Simone's name, but she did not have anything to do with telling Donna. Simone was the only one who saw him, so he wondered who told her. Jonathan said, "I saw Simone on base, so I figured she told you something about me."

"I haven't seen or heard from Simone, nor do I care to either." She sighed, "I want you out this week."

"I'm innocent."

"No, you're not, Jonathan."

"Ask Ed. He'll tell you I was at the gym."

"Ed is the one who told me you were in the dorm with some new girl."

Jonathan was floored. He couldn't believe his ears. "What?" He hoped she was making it up. His boy Ed? Why would he do this? "Ed would never tell you that."

Donna sighed and shook her head, "Dude, the look you saw between me and Terrance was because

Terrance has been trying to convince me that Ed has been lying to me. Ed has been telling me things about you for a while now. How do you think I knew you were in the bar with Simone? About the twin on the ship? I'm guessing the girl in the dorm is the same twin from the ship."

"Stop, stop. Why would Ed do this to me? I haven't done anything to him."

"Have you?" Jonathan thought but he could not remember doing anything to Ed. Donna continued. "I couldn't understand why he was coming on to me. He knew I would never fall prey to him, but the more he tried, the more I realized it was about something else. I didn't just get lucky and find out about you and Simone. Ed left me breadcrumbs that led straight to the two of you."

"I don't believe that, Donna."

"It's true. I didn't realize it was him until Erica found out."

"How long has he been hitting on you?"

"After I found out about you and Simone. He sent roses to my job and asked me to have dinner with him. He said you wouldn't be home and I could get a sitter."

"Did you go out with him?"

"I'm not a cheater. No, I didn't go out with him. In fact, I told him loyalty meant a lot to me and even though he was loyal to you in covering your tracks, that was still loyalty. The fact, that he was telling me about you meant not only was he a cheater, he was disloyal as well."

Jonathan sat on the bed. He could not believe the man he trusted was the one who was telling Donna all the information. *"At Least I will have Lea in my life. She wanted me anyway. What am I going to do with my kids?"* He asked, "What about the kids?"

"I will give you full visitation rights, but I expect child support."

"I will give you all the child support I can. I'm sorry I couldn't live up to my promise."

"Are you sorry that Ed told on you, or are you truly sorry you couldn't control your lust?"

"Both, I guess."

"Why do you feel the need to be with other women when you have a woman at home? I do everything for you, Jonathan."

"I know. I think it comes from my upbringing. To be a man, you had to sleep with as many girls as you could. I lost my virginity on a dare. I'm sorry, but I can't control myself."

"You need help. Be out by Friday."

She left the room. Jonathan pondered his fate. Now he was headed back to the single life. There was a pool of women waiting for him, but all he could think about was Lea. The pain of losing Donna was not as strong as he imagined it would be, but he guessed it was because Lea would be waiting for him. He grabbed some clothes and got a room in lodging. Maybe Lea would join him there.

He packed his gym bag, and Donna rejoined him in the room. She said, "So you're leaving tonight?"

"I am. No sense staying here if you want me out. For the record, all you have is Ed's word, and apparently, that's worth more than mine."

"Are you really going to stand there and deny you were with someone this morning?"

"You know, I was with someone this morning, but it was because I suspected you and Terrance had something going on behind my back. I was angry that you gave me so much grief over my past, but you were doing your dirt, too."

"How do you feel now knowing that's not true?"

"I actually don't feel that bad." Jonathan felt full of himself. "I thought I would hate myself for losing you, but I don't feel that bad about it. Our relationship lacked any excitement. All we did was work and come home. We would feed the kids, play with them, put them to bed, then start the cycle all over the next day. I need a woman who will bring some excitement into my life."

"I see. I hope she gives you all you need."

Jonathan threw his bag over his shoulder and headed for the front the door. "Are you going to turn us in?"

"Nope. I just want my divorce without any issues from you."

"You got it." He walked out the door, leaving his wife of only a week alone with their kids. He never imagined this happening, but he never imagined someone like Lea coming into his life. She was everything to him. He thought about the fun they would have as a couple, and for the first time in his life, he would be with someone and not feel the need to cheat.

Jonathan arrived at the base and got his room in lodging for the evening. He had money stashed away for a rainy day. It was storming in his life so the money would help him get an apartment. He hoped Lea would move in with him. However, all of that needed to wait. He had business to attend to first. Jonathan tossed his bag on the bed and headed to the dorm.

Jonathan arrived at Terrance's room and opened the door. He never knocked. If Terrance needed privacy, the door would be locked. Terrance sat on his bed. He grinned when he saw Jonathan. "What's up, boy? What are you doing on base this late?"

"Donna threw me out."

"What?"

"Why didn't you tell me Ed was telling her about me?"

"I honestly thought he would stop. He promised me he would, and I never thought Donna would believe him. I told her a thousand times that you didn't do any of the stuff, Ed said. I thought she was listening."

"I went to see Lea this morning. Ed was to be my cover. He was going to tell her I was at the gym with him. Instead, he told her I was lying, and I was in the dorm with a woman." Jonathan paused, "She caught me in a lie, so I confessed. He set me up, dude. I'm going to kick his butt."

"Don't do that, man. You will go down for adultery and assault."

Jonathan knew Terrance was right. He could not assault Ed because it would blow back on him. "Why did Ed do this to me? I never did anything to him."

Terrance laughed. "How soon we forget."

"Meaning?"

"Have you forgotten how you got Simone?"

"He's mad about that? She didn't want him."

Terrance popped his lips, "Dude, she may not have loved Ed, but she was kind of warming up to him. When you put the moves on her, she forgot all about Ed. He was pissed for weeks."

"I know he was mad, but I thought it was all a joke. I thought he never wanted her. Remember how he used to talk down about her like she was nothing?"

Terrance nodded, "One thing you never paid attention to with Ed was that he wore his emotions on his shoulders. He pretended to be hardcore like us, but inside, he loved Simone. He told me he wanted to marry her someday."

"What? How come I never heard any of that?"

"You were running around with Donna at the same time, man. You only came around to get a shot at Simone. When you weren't with either of them, you were busy being the star of the basketball team. I was here in the dorm hearing all this stuff from Ed. He hated you, man. I tried to mend the fence with us, but in hindsight, I guess I should have told you about his anger."

"Yeah, you should have. I trusted that dude and all he was trying to do was screw my wife."

"To Donna's credit, she wouldn't have any of it. She may be boring, but she's a woman you can trust."

"Well, I got me a woman I can trust. Her name is Lea, and I'm on my way to see her now."

Terrance popped up and smiled. He slapped five with Jonathan, "Now, that's my boy. Nothing holds you down."

"You know, I don't feel bad about losing Donna."

"As well you shouldn't, bro. She was the very definition of a goody-two-shoes; no fun at all. I don't know what you saw in her."

Jonathan laughed, "Have you forgotten how that butt looked before she had the kids? Come on man. We all wanted her at one time."

"Okay, you got a point there, but you should never have gotten her pregnant."

"I get it, but I love my daughters. Nothing will ever change that." Flashes of Chloe and Zoe rolled through his mind. Whatever happened with the divorce, he had to stay in touch with his girls. They were important to him. "Let me go over to Lea's room and see what she's up to."

"Sounds good."

Jonathan headed out of the room. The Supply dorm was across the street from Terrance's dorm, so he left his car parked at Terrance's dorm and walked over to Lea's room. He knocked on the door and she answered. "Well, isn't this a surprise? Come on inside, handsome."

Jonathan walked in. The room was still in a mess, but he did not mind. He embraced her soft ebony body and planted a kiss squarely on her lips. "Remember, you asked me earlier about divorcing my wife?"

"I do."

"Well, she threw me out."

"Really?"

"Yep. One of my best friends has been diming me out to her. He was my cover this morning. I told her the cover story that I was at the gym with Ed, and he told her that wasn't true and that I was in the dorm with a woman. I couldn't really deny it after that."

"Wow, some friend."

"Yep, and he was the one I thought I could trust."

"You said his name is Ed?"

"Yeah, why?"

"He was just here. He told me so much stuff about you, but I didn't believe any of it. Nor did I care. But now I'm glad I didn't believe it."

"He was trying to get with you?"

Lea smiled and sat on the bed, "Yes, he was, but I learned that if a man is tossing another man under the bus, then it's not a good place for me to be. I asked him to get out, and he left."

"Good. So, look, I have some money stashed away that my wife didn't know about. I'm getting my own apartment. How would you like to move in with me?"

"Wow, that's a big step and one that would get us both in trouble."

"I mean after the divorce. Donna is filing tomorrow. If we do it ourselves without any contest, we can be divorced in ten days to two weeks. After that, you can move in with me."

Lea crossed her legs, thinking about it. She looked up at Jonathan. "You see how I live, and I don't play games. I play around with married men because I don't want to be controlled. I can be a good girlfriend, a loyal girlfriend, but the moment I feel like I'm being controlled, I run. Are you ready for the full-time version of me, Jonathan… better yet, can you handle the full-time version of me?"

"I can, and I'm excited to have the opportunity. My wife is boring. I felt like I had no life there. With you, I know it will be different. We're going to have a great time together."

"Okay, dude, then let's try it."

Jonathan sat beside her and put his arm around her. "Tomorrow, after work, we can look at a few places. What time do you get off?"

"I get off at 4:30."

"So do I. I will pick you up from here at five."

"We have to be careful, honey. Your wife might come for you… us."

"She won't. She knows if I get in trouble, it will cost her money. Donna is very smart. She'll just divorce me, but she would never mess with her own money."

"Smart girl."

"That she is. Now let's get it on."

GERALD C. ANDERSON, SR.

"Okay, Marvin Gaye."

Chapter 8

Jonathan's day at work progressed well. He could not get his mind off the night he spent with Lea. She made his world, and he thought no more about Donna. He wanted to face Ed, but Terrance talked him out of it. For now, his meeting with Lea to search for their new apartment was all he wanted to do.

Jonathan rushed out of the legal office and went to his lodging room. He changed out of his uniform, then made his way to Lea's room. She was standing on the balcony waiting for him. When she came down, Jonathan opened the car door for her with a smiled. She pinched his cheek and patted him on the face. Jonathan became a victim of his own rule… he had caught feelings.

As he was driving off the base, he saw Donna heading home with the kids. For a minute, he missed them. He reminisced about the times he would walk through the door, and they would greet him. Those moments were worth more than money. Then he looked into Lea's eyes and forgot about them.

The couple arrived at a townhouse Lea discovered was up for rent. She wanted to look at it because her friend lived in the community, and she loved it. Jonathan noticed the outside of the community was beautiful and looked expensive. He asked, "Are you sure we can afford this?"

"I know I won't be getting BAQ or VHA, but with your income and mine, we can do it, baby. I have a line number for tech sergeant too. That will bring extra money when I sew it on."

Her confidence and the sound of love from her voice inspired him. They got out of the car and the landlord greeted them. "Hi, are you the couple interested in renting the townhouse?"

Jonathan answered, "Yes, that would be us."

"Great, let me show you the place." They walked inside and the kitchen was immediately to the left. "Here is your kitchen. The appliances are brand new. Women love the design of the kitchen. This island in the middle here is very helpful when preparing food."

Lea said, "I'm sold."

They all laughed, then Jonathan said, "Maybe we should look at the rest of the house."

The landlord replied, "And that's typically what the man says." They laughed again, and the landlord showed them around the townhouse. Jonathan loved it, but he was concerned about the deposit and the rent. He had enough to cover the deposit, but he did not know how they would furnish it. The landlord said, "So, are we going to rent it?"

Lea quickly responded, "Yes!"

Jonathan said, "Wait, can we have a minute to chat?"

The landlord answered, "Sure, I'll step outside for a smoke."

He left and Jonathan said, "Lea, baby, this is a great place. I have the deposit money, but what about furniture? Donna gets to keep all our stuff."

She placed her soft hands on each of Jonathan's shoulders, "Honey, we can get furniture. I know a place that will allow you to pay on it. They will give us a loan if we both sign up."

"You're so confident in all of this."

"Look, I can't put my name on the lease because the Air Force won't give me the money like you're getting, but let me help with the furniture." Jonathan thought about it. Inside, he wondered for a moment if he would be stuck with a lease he could not pay for. Lea continued, "Jonathan, don't you believe in us? I do. I believe we're made for each other and one day we will get married. Let's do this, baby."

He pondered some more. The words Lea spoke soothed his spirit. Inside, he believed he made the right choice in leaving Donna for Lea. The concern of her not wanting to be on the lease was a good one since it would give the Air Force reason to investigate them. Being a paralegal, he knew that better than anyone. "Okay Lea, I have faith in you, baby. Let's do this."

She jumped up. "Yes! I love you, baby."

Jonathan thought, *"Wow, love already! Could it be that she really loves me? I don't know, but I'm excited about it."* Jonathan replied, "Yes, baby, I love you too. Let's go talk to that landlord." They walked outside and discussed the details with the landlord. After Jonathan signed the lease, they went to the furniture store and signed the loan papers for the furniture. In one evening, Jonathan put Donna behind him and started a life with Lea. They headed back to the base, where they ran into Donna in the lodging parking lot.

Lea stayed in the car. Jonathan approached Donna. "What are you doing here?"

"I came to give you these."

"You had the papers drawn up that fast?"

"I did. Get her out of the car."

"What?"

"I don't think I stuttered Jonathan. Get her out of the car." Jonathan went to the car and asked Lea to get out. They both joined Donna near Donna's car. "So you're the one who my husband couldn't resist. It's nice to meet you again." Lea nodded and turned her head to the side. "Anyway, I have the divorce papers completed. I've signed them and you can sign them in front of a notary. You know how that works since you work in legal."

"Okay, not a problem."

"The document is per our conversation. You have visitation every other weekend and every other Wednesday. Of course, I don't mind if you want them at a time outside of that. All I ask is that you let me know a day in advance."

Jonathan replied, "Thank you for that."

Donna handed Jonathan the papers. "Now, I will not turn the two of you in, so you don't have to worry about that. I don't want you to get an Article 15 that would cause you to lose your stripes. I mean, that would cut off myself since I would get less child support. However, I hope you two will keep your relationship on the down low. They projected our court date to be two weeks away. I'm sure you should be able to maintain yourselves until then."

"Don't worry about us."

"Oh, I'm not worried. You're an expert with this." She popped her lips, "As you for Lea, if you harm my kids in any way, I will bury your behind."

"I don't have anything to do with your kids."

"You're with their father. You will have something to do with my kids." Lea rolled her eyes at

Donna. Donna continued, "This is the woman you picked over me? If she mistreats my children, I will come for you."

"They are my kids too and I wouldn't have anyone around them who would hurt them."

Donna replied, "I will be watching. Your visitation starts the weekend after next." Donna got inside her car and pulled off.

Lea asked, "How did she know you were here?"

"I told her in case something happened to my kids."

The look on Lea's face said she was not happy. Jonathan took her to eat, then back to her room. He wanted to stay the night with her, but Donna was right. They needed to lay low until the divorce went through.

Jonathan went to Terrance's room. Terrance was standing on the balcony. "Hey, man, I saw you drop off Lea. You better lay low because the ball and chain might turn you in."

"She won't. She just told both of us she won't because if I get demoted, she'll lose money in child support."

Terrance snapped his fingers, "Makes sense to me. So, what have you been up to?"

"Just signed this lease to a townhouse and got some furniture. We… I move on Friday."

"Wow, man, this is all happening so fast! Just a few days ago, you were the devoted husband. Now you're moving into your own place and getting a divorce. Man, I'm so not getting married."

"Hey, this wouldn't be happening if it weren't for Ed."

Terrance shook his head, "You're right, but I should have told you what he was up to."

"Have you seen him?"

"I've seen him, but he doesn't talk to me. He's a punk in my eyes."

"Same here."

Terrance said, "I saw Simone. You know if she finds out you're going to be single again, she might want to get some."

Jonathan laughed, "No, this time I'm going to be faithful. I need to change, man. My lustful behavior cost me my family. Lucky for me, I got a woman like Lea. I'm going to do right this time."

Terrance grinned, "Unless Simone wants you. Dude, you're like me. If they offer it up, you're going to take it. That's why I'm not married."

"Not this time, man."

"You miss Donna?"

"I don't. I should have never been with Donna. She's a good woman, too good for the likes of me, but I need a spirited woman like Lea. I need someone living

118

life on the edge. Someone that brings excitement in the relationship. With Donna, you know what you're going to get. I never have to worry about where she is, what she's doing, nothing. She's dependable and reliable."

Mike Hollinger joined them on the balcony. Terrance said, "Speaking of dependable and reliable."

Mike said, "What's up, fellas?"

Terrance said, "What's up, Mike?"

Jonathan added, "What going on, brother?"

Mike answered, "Nothing, but I heard about you, Jonathan. Ed sold you out to your wife."

Terrance said, "Yeah, he's a punk."

Jonathan added, "Yeah, that's not how a brother is supposed to roll."

Mike said, "Hey, man, Donna is a great catch. I don't understand why you played her like that. I really don't understand why she stayed with you for so long."

Jonathan answered, "The reason I stayed with her was because of the kids. She got pregnant from our first time, so I felt locked in from the beginning. I don't know if I even loved her."

Mike shook his head, "Dude, you loved her. The problem with guys like you is you don't appreciate what you have until it's gone."

Jonathan stepped back, "What? She's gone and I don't even miss her. What does that tell you?"

"It tells me you haven't realized that you lost a good thing yet. I heard about you and the new girl in Supply. She's masking the pain for you."

Jonathan laughed, "Really, dude? You're a loyal brother who wouldn't play a woman if your life depended on it, but you're not married. Are you even dating anyone?"

Mike hesitated. "No, I'm not married, but it's because I'm waiting for the right one to come along. As for dating, I am talking to someone. I'll see where it goes."

Terrance laughed, "If it doesn't go to sex inside a month, it's a waste."

Mike chuckled, "That's the wrong attitude, brother."

Terrance asked, "So how long you plan on waiting?"

"I won't have sex with her until I'm married."

Terrance and Jonathan burst out laughing. Jonathan said, "Dude, I would have kept that to myself."

"I have nothing to be ashamed of. I tried it your way, but it got me nowhere. You fall in love with sex and not the person. I want to fall in love with the person. Sex will be the icing on the cake after marriage. Waiting until my wedding night will be perfect for both of us."

Terrance said, "Whew, I thought he was about to say he was a virgin, Jonathan. That would have been it for me."

"No, brother, I've been out there, but I learned my lesson. Something you both should do before you get hurt."

Jonathan laughed, "Hurt? Man, there is not a woman on Earth that could hurt me."

Terrance high fived Jonathan, "Don't you know it."

Mike said, "You guys have to live and learn. I'm off to church."

Jonathan replied, "Oh, that explains it. You're one of them brothers."

"Yep, and proud of it." He walked away, leaving Jonathan and Terrance alone. Jonathan continued to peer out over the balcony, watching the cars go by. He wanted to go see Lea, but headed back to his room instead. *Today was good and soon me and Lea will live together. Then, two weeks from now, I'll be single and able to be out and in the open with my new lady.*

Chapter 9

Thursday afternoon, happy hour social at the NCO Club was an ongoing weekly event for the base. Many of the airmen and NCOs hung out there. Jonathan and Terrance were among them. Ed was also at the event, but across the room from them. Jonathan stared at him with cold eyes. Terrance reminded him it would not be good to start a fight in a place where several chief master sergeants were hanging out. Jonathan said, "Look at that punk over there laughing like a little girl."

"Come on, man, this place is filled with some of the sexiest military girls in the world, and you're looking at a dude? I'm worrying about you, my friend."

"I'm good, man. I'm just focused on my girl. You know Lea told me she loved me the other day."

Terrance choked on his drink. "What, she uttered the words."

"Tell me you didn't say it back."

"Yeah, I did."

"Dude! This is the same thing I told you about Donna. Don't go down this road. These girls are made for having a little fun. Don't fall in love with them. Me, I won't fall in love with anyone until I've finished sowing all my oats, and I have so many more to go. Look at that hot red bone over there."

Jonathan looked in the direction Terrance was looking. "She's hot, but she's married and has three kids."

"You scouted her already?"

"No, her husband played ball with me before he started night school. He's a cool dude. I don't know how he stays chained to one woman, but some dudes can do it. I guess you'll be saying that about me next."

"I'll believe it when I see it."

Jonathan chuckled, "Man, I'm serious. I'm not cheating anymore. Lea is going to be my wife and I will be her man forever. No more side-pieces."

"Didn't you say that about Donna a couple of weeks ago?"

"I was living in fear then. I just didn't want to lose my kids, but Donna did nothing to keep me from wondering. The same old basic sex got boring."

Terrance popped his lips, "Yeah, see that chick over there with Sergeant Billings?"

"Yeah, Monica, right?"

"Yeah, I thought she was hot. Dude, boring. I mean she put the 'b' in boring. I tried to do some things with her, and she wasn't into it all. One and done."

Jonathan laughed, "It's funny how we compare notes and cover a good number of the girls in this area."

"Because we dogs, bruh. We know it and we don't care."

"I know, man."

They slapped five. Terrance continued, "Dude, heads up; your girl's coming."

"Lea?"

Terrance said, "Yep. Hey, Lea. How are you?"

"I'm good and you?"

"I'm doing good. I'll get out of you guys' way. I see a girl that wants to get to know me."

Jonathan laughed, "Settle down, bro." Terrance nodded and headed for someone he was interest in. "So, should we be seen like this in public?"

"We're just at the club like everyone else. There's nothing wrong with that."

Jonathan smiled, "You're so pretty."

"Thank you. Are you ready for tomorrow?"

"I am."

"I'm moving some of my stuff, but not all of it. I will move all of it after your divorce is final."

"That will be in eight days."

Lea smiled, leaned back, and crossed her legs. "I can't wait either."

Jonathan looked up and Erica walked in. She looked at Jonathan and rolled her eyes. She could not stand him as much as he could not stand her. Lea asked, "Who is that?"

"Erica Young. She thinks she's all that and a bag of chips. I got news for her; she ain't."

"One of Donna's friends."

"Yes."

"I'm out. I'll see you tomorrow night, sweetie."

Jonathan stood, "Wait, have a drink."

Lea turned, "Nope." She walked straight for the exit.

Jonathan knew she was concerned about her career. He was concerned too, but inside he was more in love with her than he will admit. He looked over at Ed, who was now sitting with Erica. He wanted to punch him in the face. Terrance rejoined him. "Lea didn't look happy."

"She wasn't. She's concerned about Erica and what she might say to Donna."

"I don't blame her. Erica is a 'b'."

"That's an understatement." Jonathan looked around to see who might be looking. "I'll catch you later, man. I'm going home to get my stuff together for tomorrow."

"Okay, Bro. Have a good evening."

Jonathan rose, "You too, man. Good luck in here."

"Hmm, I'm going to need it."

Jonathan walked away laughing. He knew Terrance did not know when to cut his losses and settle down with someone. Over the last three years, the entire base became familiar with their doggish antics. Now no one would go out with him. They warned the new women before he could make a move. Jonathan was thankful that he had Lea. If he lost Donna without having someone on the side, he would be lost, too.

He returned to his room and packed his bags. He felt the excitement of moving into his own place with the woman he loved. Jonathan never felt the love he now felt for Lea. He missed Chloe and Zoe, and he would get them the first weekend he was divorced. He hoped Lea would be okay with the girls. He never asked her opinion on kids, but made a conscience note to ask the next day.

When he was done with packing, he laid in the bed and imagined his life with Lea. He dreamed of them having a long life together with kids. Before he knew it, sleep overtook him.

The sound of the alarm slammed into his ears, waking him from a good dream. He thought, *"Why is it the good dreams that end with the alarm going off? Man, I have a long day ahead of me."* He forced himself to get up and get cleaned up. He had to work half the day, and he wanted to get as much done before he needed to meet the landlord at the townhouse. The furniture would be delivered around four that afternoon. Lea would be there at six. He wanted them to have a great dinner and an even better evening alone.

Jonathan grabbed a coffee and headed to work. He arrived at his desk in the Military Justice section. His supervisor, Master Sergeant Miller, told him he could get off at noon, but he needed to finish the court documents for a case the next week. As soon as he sat at his desk, the phone rang. "Military Justice, Sergeant Rose, may I help you?"

"So one week to go as a married man."

"Simone, I thought I heard the last of you."

"Nope. I also heard you found out who was feeding Donna her information. I thought I would help you out by calling you so you could apologize to me."

"Really, Simone?"

"Yes, really. I told you I wasn't telling her anything."

"I'm sorry. How's that?"

"It will do. I wonder if Lea knows what she's getting herself into?"

"Lea and I have a special relationship. She was the one I should have waited for all my life."

Simone burst into laughter, "You've got to be kidding me, dude. I was the best thing you had, but you didn't appreciate me. And… I'm no Donna Rose fan, but she's much better than what you got now."

"Look, I have work to do, Simone. Have a nice day."

"You too. I can't wait to see this blow up in your face. I'm going to be right there to make sure you know it."

"Whatever; goodbye." He hung up the phone, annoyed by Simone and her comments. He knew she was angry that they broke up, but she needed to get over it. Jonathan's life with Lea would be great and no one could tell him otherwise.

Jonathan finished up his paperwork. The noon hour arrived, and he changed clothes in the bathroom. The excitement of a new life filled his spirit. Rushing to his car, he headed to the townhouse to sign the final documents and get the key. He'd waited for this day to come, but cursed himself for not calling Lea. He was dedicated to her, but he chastised himself for not doing the little things like calling her before he left. She told him she had training in the afternoon, so he missed his window to call. *"Oh well, she'll be fine."*

Jonathan arrived at the townhouse and met with the landlord. All the paperwork was in order, and he signed for the townhouse. Receiving the keys was one of the best moments of his life. When he signed the paperwork for the duplex he lived in with Donna, they both signed the lease. It was a team effort for everything they did, but Jonathan did not feel like the man because he needed Donna's help. This time, he did it on his own. He poked out his chest after he signed the papers, feeling like the man.

Soon, the furniture arrived. Everything was in order. Jonathan thought, *"Everything is in place. Only one more piece to this happy puzzle… Lea. Come on baby, let's get this party started."*

Jonathan was busy getting things situated when Lea arrived. He was not sure how she would want everything, but he started anyway. The knock at the door startled him. He regained his composure and answered it. "Hey, lady. I've been waiting for you."

"Really, I never got a call."

"I was busy getting the court paperwork ready for next week. When I got off, I remembered you were in training."

She rolled her eyes at him, "It's the little things that count."

"Yes, you are correct. I should have called, but they had me so tied up that I barely had the time to do anything."

Lea popped her lips, "Okay, help me with my stuff."

"I thought you weren't bringing everything."

"I didn't." She turned and smiled at him as they retrieved her things from the car.

Jonathan and Lea cuddled in the bed, sipping wine. Jonathan could not imagine himself in a better place. Now all he needed was his divorce to go through so he could show the world his love for Lea. She looked at him with her beautiful hazel eyes, and he knew his love was locked away in her heart. He needed no other woman but Lea. He said, "You got something on your mind?"

Lea answered, "Mia called me today. She said Ray committed suicide because she told him it was off."

"Wow, that brother was bad off."

"Yeah, he went passed catching feelings. My sister was very depressed but I told her it's not her fault. She can't stay with a man because he may take his life. That would be prison for her."

"Did she tell anyone he might be suicidal?"

"No, she didn't think he was."

"That's sad."

Lea turned to him, "Anyway, are you ready for another round?"

"You know I am, baby."

She laid back and opened her legs allowing Jonathan entrance into her. Jonathan said, "There's no better moment than a woman granting entrance into her body. You're all I need, baby."

"I better be." She smiled that seductive smile that got him hooked on the ship. It felt like their life together spanned years when it was merely weeks. The more he progressed in making love to her, the louder her screams of joy became.

"Yes, this is what I want from my woman. Let me know you love it!" His manhood was refreshed. She gave him what he needed, the excitement he wanted. He said, "Shout, baby. Tell me you love it!"

She shouted loud, "I love it!" The scream was so loud the neighbors pounded on the wall. Jonathan and Lea laughed.

Before long, Lea was fast asleep. Jonathan got up because he heard a sound downstairs. He walked down the steps being careful but found nothing. He remembered how his stepdad used to be up at night creeping around the house. *"Now that's me."* He laughed at himself. Then he noticed Lea's purse on the table. A notebook had fallen out of it. He went to put it back inside her purse when he noticed something written on the inside cover. It was only six digits, but he wondered if she left the seventh one off in case he found the notebook. The numbers in reverse order were Terrance's phone number without the last digit and area code. Jonathan was anal when it came to numbers and data. He could spot a pattern faster than most people. *"Must be a coincidence. Why would she go through this much trouble to disguise his number? The odds of me finding this notebook were slim to none."* He closed the notebook, tucked it back in her purse, and went back upstairs.

Jonathan watched her sleeping. It was a beautiful sight to him. He never took so much care with Donna, and now he realized why. He did not love Donna like he loved Lea. Lea stirred, so Jonathan moved in for another round of love.

Chapter 10

The Judge said, "Having found no reason for this marriage to continue, I grant the dissolution of marriage submitted by Donna Rose and hereby proclaim this marriage dissolved."

Jonathan thought he would be happy at the announcement, but something ate at him. He watched Donna celebrate with Erica and Rene and wondered if he made a mistake. Did he let the best thing for him go? He reasoned he was out of his mind and that no one wants to go through a divorce. He chalked the feelings up to the experience of divorce.

He got into his car and drove back to the townhouse. Lea was working, but he called her. There was no answer on her cell. He texted her saying he was a single man and they would have to celebrate. A few moments later she replied, asking how they could if he had the kids this weekend.

"Wow, she has a problem with my children." He texted he could get them the next weekend if it was going to be a problem. She replied t it would not be and that she would see him after work. Jonathan asked her if she wanted to go to lunch and she replied saying she had training for the rest of the day. Jonathan sighed and called his boy Terrance. "Hey yo, T, what's up, bro?"

"Obviously, it went well and you're a single man now, right?"

"That I am, bro. Let's do lunch."

"Ah, man, I can't. If you had called me a few minutes ago, I could have gone."

"Dang, man. I can't find anyone to celebrate with."

"You called Lea?"

"Yeah, she said she's got training."

"Oh wow, sorry bro. Just chill at home until she comes back. Then you can celebrate."

"I think she doesn't want the kids around. I mentioned celebrating and she brought them up like they would be in the way. I don't know what's going to happen there."

"Give her some time, man. You're asking her to go from single with no kids to shacking up with two kids."

"You're right. I'll tell Donna my week needs to start next week."

"I think you should stick to the schedule. Don't give Donna a reason to get anything started."

"You have a point there."

"Anyway, I got to roll out, man. Have fun. Get some stuff ready for tonight."

"Yes, sir." He hung up the phone. An unknown text popped up on his phone. It read, *"Now the fun begins. Maybe you should take a ride over to the Supply dorm."* Jonathan did not understand what the message meant. He pondered if he should go or not. It was after 11 and Lea would be home at five. If he cleaned the house and made dinner, she would be happy. He figured he would roll out to the dorm and see if the message meant anything or not, then he would come back and cook and clean.

Jonathan got himself together. It took him longer than he expected, but he left the house and headed to the base. When he arrived at the Supply dorm, there was nothing out of the ordinary. *"Figured someone was pulling my chain. I don't know what people are trying to prove, but it didn't work."* Jonathan believed he knew who sent him the text. He called her, "What are you trying to prove?"

"Jonathan, I don't know what you're talking about, but what time are you getting the kids?"

"I will pick them up at five, but don't think I don't know it's you with the texts."

"Texts? I haven't sent you any texts, Jonathan. Be here at five."

She hung up the phone. Donna became colder with each day. She wanted nothing to do with Jonathan. He knew her dream was to get married and stay married her entire life. Because of him, that did not work. Another text came through, *You took too long to get there.*

Jonathan texted back, *Who are you and what are you trying to show me?* There was no response. Jonathan drove off and headed back home to cook and clean. Tonight was going to be special, no matter what.

The evening came. Jonathan cooked and played with the kids while Lea sat in the bedroom. She stayed away from the girls. Jonathan felt pressure to decide between his children and his new girlfriend. The life he imagined was not going as he expected. After dinner, Jonathan cleaned up the dishes, then put the kids to bed. Afterwards, he walked into the bedroom, where Lea waited. She rushed to put her phone away as if she were hiding something.

Jonathan asked, "What's up? Are you hiding something?"

"Nope, just getting ready for this long awaited celebration."

That comment made Jonathan happy. He pulled back the covers and realized she was naked. Jonathan salivated. The celebration would take his mind completely off the way Lea treated his girls. After the moments of pleasure were over, then he would discuss the matter with her. For now, his focus was on getting laid.

The sex seemed to last forever to Jonathan. He rolled over and licked his lips, "Baby, I think you dried me out."

"It's not my fault you stayed down there so long." She giggled. "But I loved it."

Jonathan laughed, "I heard." Lea joined him in laughing. The fun times made Jonathan feel vindicated in divorcing his wife.

Lea asked, "Do you want me to get you some water?"

"Sure, I can use a drink." Lea walked out of the bedroom. Jonathan was satisfied beyond any doubt. He forgot the treatment his daughters received that evening and deal with it another day. Keeping the children away from Lea seemed best. When he had them, he would spend time with them somewhere else. Maybe one day Lea would decide to join them. In the meantime, he wanted nothing to come between their love.

Her phone beeped. She left it sitting on the nightstand while she went to get water, something she rarely did. Curiosity got the best of him, and he looked at the name. It said, CD for the name and the message read, *"Coming out?"* Jonathan wondered if she was seeing someone on the side. His emotions flipped from happiness to concern. He thought, *"I wonder if this is how Donna felt?"* Lea returned to the room and handed him a glass of water. Jonathan said, "Your phone beeped." Her face changed.

She looked at the phone without saying a word, then laughed, "It's from Cherrie. I met her earlier this week. She wants me to come to the club, but I told her we were celebrating your divorce." She put the phone in her purse and got in the bed. Lea cuddled with Jonathan, and that familiar sensation came into his spirit. He did the same thing with Donna.

Morning arrived, and the tiny knock at his room door sounded familiar. Lea pushed him in the shoulder. "Your kids are knocking at the door."

"You could have opened it for them."

"Whatever."

Jonathan rolled his eyes at her and opened the door. Chloe and Zoe hugged his legs. "Good morning daddy!" Their words fixed a ton of problems in his life. They would love him no matter what.

He hugged them both and asked, "You guys hungry?" They both said yes, and Jonathan took them downstairs to make breakfast. "How about pancakes?"

"Yes!"

"You guys always talk in union?"

Chloe asked, "What's unison?"

"Never mind." He laughed at his girls. They made his life. Lea joined them downstairs and hugged Jonathan.

"Hey, sorry about the comment. You're right. I could have answered the door." She turned to Chloe and Zoe, "So girls, would you guys like to go to the park later?"

They both jumped up and said yes. Jonathan smiled. She was trying, and that's all he wanted. After breakfast, Jonathan got the girls dressed. He put them in the same outfits so they would match. Donna wanted them to be individuals, but Jonathan loved making them look like twins. His cell beeped with a text. It was another mysterious text. This time, it told him he was a fool for losing a good thing. *"Who is this? Donna doesn't have the skills to do this."*

Lea came into the girl's room. "You dressed them the same?"

"Yeah, they're twins."

"I used to hate it when our parents dressed us the same."

Jonathan dropped his head. "Not you too."

"Donna felt the same?"

"Yes."

"She's right." Lea walked out. One thing that was certain about Lea was she said her piece and did not wait around for an answer or an argument.

139

Jonathan and the girls met Lea at the door. Jonathan noticed Lea was dressed in shorts that would make any man want to cheat. He was proud to have her on his arm as his woman and the world could know it.

They took the kids to the park. Jonathan became annoyed with the text messages. Someone was harassing him, and it had to stop. He knew someone who worked in technology and hoped he could help him figure out who's sending the texts.

After the park, they took the girls to get ice cream, then headed home. Once home, Jonathan called Trey. "Hey, Trey, I got a problem that I'm hoping you can help me with."

"What's that, bro?"

"Someone is sending me texts, and it's annoying the heck out of me. I want to see if you can figure out who it is."

"I can try, but these cell phones aren't as easy as they used to be."

"Anything you can do will help, bro."

"Okay, bring me your phone in about an hour."

"Will do. I'll have my girls with me. Is that okay?"

"Sure, man. My old lady is here with our kids. They'll have fun."

"Great, see you in an hour, bro."

An hour rolled by, and Jonathan arrived at Trey's home. Trey was the best at computers, and he did some hacking on the side for clients. Jonathan and Trey went to basic training together, and Jonathan realized it would be good to befriend him. Jonathan said, "Hey bro. Here's my phone. This is the number that's texting me."

"Cool, let me check it out."

"You brought the girls?"

"Yeah, they raced over to your kids. They're probably having a ball by now."

"Yeah, dude, this is a burner number. I can tell you where it was purchased, but nothing else. Definitely can't tell you who's sending the texts."

"I figured as much. I know it's not Donna. She's not technical enough."

"Right, but all she has to do is buy a burner phone. You can pick one of them up anywhere."

"Hmm, maybe it is her then." Jonathan gave it some thought, "Hey, one more thing. Something isn't right with my new girl. She's getting texts and talking on the phone. To think of it, she's acting a lot like me when I was cheating on Donna. You got anything for that?"

"Yeah, if you get her phone, take out the SIM card and place it in this. Then you can copy her card. After it's copied replace her SIM card and now you have a copy of her SIM that will allow you to see everything she sees."

"Isn't that illegal?"

"No, because you're only cloning the card to spy. You're not copying the data to use on your device. That's illegal."

"Okay, it might be hard getting her phone. She doesn't leave it lying around."

"Does anyone? Man, if you know what I know, you will never leave your phone laying around."

"I don't. That's part of The Cheater's Code; never leave evidence lying around." They both chuckled, "Somehow I will get to the bottom of this."

"I believe you will. Sorry about you and Donna. She is a great catch."

The comment caught Jonathan by surprise. Another man felt Donna was a great catch. He wondered why he could not see it himself. "Thanks, Trey, but hey, she wasn't what everyone thought she was. I'll see you later."

"Cool, man, let me know how it turns out."

"Will do." Jonathan grabbed the girls and headed back to the townhouse. The girls were happy having played with friends they had not seen in a while. Jonathan stopped off at McDonald's and got them something to eat. They ate at McDonalds then went home. When they arrived, Lea's car was not there.

Jonathan took the girls in the house and there was a note on the dining room table. It read, *"Hey, babe, I had to run on base to see one of my girls. They are having an afternoon lunch. I'll be back soon!"*

Jonathan put the note in the trash. He did not think to question the note because Lea often hung out with her girls. He did not receive any more texts, and that was great.

Jonathan kept the girls entertained until they took a nap. He joined them in their room, having been tired himself. After an hour, he woke. The girls were still asleep and Lea was still not home. Now he questioned the note. He asked himself, *"Am I being paranoid?"*

The afternoon and evening rolled by. Jonathan made the girls bath water. After their bath, he read them a bedtime story and put them to sleep. He called Lea, but it went to voicemail. His concerned turned to anger. Moments later, she came through the door. He rolled his eyes at her, expecting a lie. His faith in her was waning. He wondered if the choice he made was horribly wrong.

"Hey, babe. Sorry I'm late but my girls wanted to hang all day. I texted you earlier. Don't be mad."

Jonathan laughed inside. It was the same thing he would say to Donna. "No worries. I just wanted to make sure you were okay." He noticed his reply was similar to what Donna would say to him. He did not believe anything she said. To copy her phone he needed to get her SIM card. It would not be easy.

The night was uneventful. Jonathan spent most of it trying to get to Lea's phone. He hated feeling this way, but that nagging feeling that she was up to something haunted him. He thought, *"I guess this is my punishment for all the years I spent dogging women. Donna must have done this so many times. I should have been better."*

Sunday morning arrived and Jonathan, Lea and the girls spent the day together at the park then the beach. It was the best day Jonathan had. It eased his worries about the relationship between Lea and the kids. They got along great.

After Jonathan dropped the girls back with Donna, he spent a quiet evening cuddling with Lea. As always, she made him feel like he was the only man in the world that mattered. He chastised himself for thinking about copying her SIM card. He fell asleep on the couch with Lea. When he woke up, she was gone. He went upstairs and heard mumbling in the bathroom. He got closer and heard her say, "No, you need to do it, and soon." She hung up the phone and opened the door. Lea jumped, seeing Jonathan standing there. "Sorry, I hope I didn't wake you?"

"No, what was that call about?"

"Nothing, just my sister. She needed some advice."

Jonathan nodded, but he did not believe a word she said. After a great day in which she made him believe he was the only man in her life, he was back to his suspicions. They laid down together. Jonathan watched her lock her phone and put it under her pillow. A strange move for anyone, but it prevented him from copying her SIM card.

Jonathan arrived at work and started his day with his favorite coffee. He loved his coffee with cream and sugar. The office phone rang, and he answered, "Military Justice, Sergeant Rose, may I help you?"

"Hey, Jonathan, the girls said they had a great time and they liked Lea. I'm glad to hear that. I was concerned about their relationship with the women you exposed them to."

"Women? There's only one woman in my life now."

"I really hope that's true, because you need to settle down and be a man."

"I've been a man. I don't need to hear this crap."

"Hey look, I didn't call to harass you, but I didn't get the check. You said it would be direct deposited today."

"It was supposed to be. I'll check with Finance and see what happened."

"Okay, take care."

"You too." Jonathan hung up the phone. *"So it begins, harassment over custody checks. I have 16 years of this mess to go."*

Work took his mind off his problems with Lea. When she called at 10, it made his morning. "Hey, Lea. How is your day going?"

"Good. I just called to ask if you wanted to go to the club for lunch?" Now that proposal was something he wanted to hear. She was asking him to lunch.

"I would love to meet my girl for lunch. What time?"

"I have to go at 11. I can meet you there."

"Sounds good, baby. I'll get there a little early so I can get us a table."

"And…"

"Order for you, baby. I got you."

"You're so awesome. I love you."

Jonathan forgot about the issues with her again. The three magical words lit up his life. "I love you too, baby. See you in an hour."

"Okay, honey. I'm counting the minutes."

"Me too." He hung up the phone with a smile on his face. If nothing else, Lea was the best at putting him at ease. He was not sure if she was cheating on him. If she was, she was the best at it.

Captain Graves walked into the office. "What's the big Kool-Aid smile for?"

"My girl. Since my divorce, it's been up and down with us, but somehow, she makes me smile. I don't know if she has a sixth sense or something, but she knows when I'm questioning our relationship and she takes measures to let me know I'm the only man in her life."

"That's a good thing."

"Tell me about it. It's better than Donna. She hounded me all the time about everything."

Captain Graves scratched his head, "Yeah, but she is a good woman. At least from what I could see. It's a shame you guys couldn't make it."

"Yeah, I'd better get this Article 15 done and to you before I head out to lunch."

"Cool. I'm supposed to get a legal assistance client, but just leave it on your desk and I'll grab it."

"Thanks, Captain." Captain Graves left Jonathan's office. He continued to work thinking about the constant reminders about how good of a woman Donna appeared to be to others, but to him she was anything but. He did not love her, and that is why he choose to be with other women.

Jonathan finished the Article 15 and headed to meet Lea. He arrived at the club and grabbed a seat in the dining area. He watched Donna and Erica come in and take a seat. She did not acknowledge him. He thought, *"I guess we've gotten to that stage now. Oh well, I traded up and here she comes. Oh, man. Can she get any finer?"* Jonathan stood up and pulled the seat out for Lea. She sat down with that seductive smile she always wore just for him.

"So, I see your ex is in the building with her stank BFF."

Jonathan laughed, "Yeah, she didn't speak to me either. She looked right at me and turned away. I knew Erica wouldn't speak. She's hated me since day one."

"Do you care?"

"Heck no. I've got the best-looking woman in the world. Why would I care?"

"You know my twin sister would argue with that, right?"

Jonathan laughed, "Beauty is more than what's seen by the eye. That's where you have her beat."

"Oh, baby, you keep this up and you'll get some tonight."

"Then let me keep it going then."

Lea twisted her head, "Don't be giving me none of those lines that you used on those other women."

"I created new lines for the queen of my heart. Those lines were just to get them. I need lines to keep you... forever!"

Lea's head snapped back, "Forever? Jonathan, are you trying to find out if I'm interested in tying the knot?"

"Maybe." The server arrived and took their drink and food order. Jonathan noticed Terrance come into the dining area. He waved at Jonathan, and Jonathan waved back. Lea looked at him and for an instance there was a stare between the two of them. Jonathan watched Terrance closely to see if anything was revealed.

Lea snapped her fingers, "Are you having lunch with me or your best friend?"

"I'm sorry. There seems to be a change in Terrance. I'm not sure what it is, but something is different about him."

"Jealous maybe?"

"Why do you say that?"

"Come on, Jonathan. Haven't you noticed how he looks at me? He wants me and he's mad you got me. From what I heard, he's still mad that you got Simone too."

"Why would he be mad about that? That's why Ed fell out with me and told Donna what I was up to. They both wanted Simone, but she wanted me."

149

"This Simone girl must have been something special. All of you wanted her."

Jonathan did not dare answer the question. It was a no-win question for him. "Simone was cool, but I don't know why they are so in an uproar over her. She's available now, but they aren't moving on her."

"How do you know they're not? You don't talk to Ed anymore, right?'

"No, I don't, but people talk, and they say she's seeing some guy downtown."

Lea shrugged her shoulders, "Oh, well good for her. Anyway, I wanted to have this lunch with my man to talk about us, not them."

Jonathan felt a pit in his stomach. He wondered if she was about to dump him. "Okay, what's wrong?"

"Why does something have to be wrong?"

"I don't know. People typically have meetings when things are going bad, not when they are going well."

"Well, Jonathan, boo…" She laughed, "This meeting is a good meeting. I just wanted to tell you I'm happy and in love."

Her words struck deep into Jonathan's heart. He looked into her eyes and wanted to ask her to marry him then, but he had no ring to give her. "Baby, I love you too, and I'm happy." He reached across the table and grabbed her hand. "I know we're still feeling each other out, but I know we are destined for a long future together."

Lea squirmed in her seat, "Let's not rush things too much now. I'm into you and I want this to last, but we have to take our time about marriage."

Those were words Jonathan did not want to hear. He wanted to lock her down so no one else could have a shot at her. "Okay, but I am so into you, Lea, that even I can't believe the change in me. I've never been so dedicated to a woman before." Jonathan noticed the worried look on Lea's face. "Hey look, I apologize for getting too mushy. Let's just enjoy our food."

Lea folded her lips inward, "Okay."

The couple continued to eat their lunch. Afterwards Jonathan walked Lea to her car, and she headed back to work. Once inside his car, he pondered the look on her face. Part of him believed she loved him, but she was not ready to settle down. He wondered if she was still out there. Were his suspicions legitimate? He enjoyed the sweet words she said, but the looks when he hinted at marriage bothered him. Most of all, he was concerned when she looked worried because he admitted his dedication to her.

After work, Jonathan walked to his car. Simone pulled up and stepped out of her car. "Jonathan, how's it going, dude?"

"Very well, and you?"

"I'm living my best life. You are head-over-heels in love, I hear. I don't believe it myself."

"What is this about, Simone?"

She snickered, "Look, I was mad at you for what you did to me."

"What I did to you? You knew I was with Donna, so what did I do to you?"

"You told me you would leave her and be with me? You forgot about that?"

He had not forgotten about that. He would have said anything to get with her. Jonathan remembered telling more women than he could count that lie; knowing it was never true. He said, "Okay, I'll give you that. I'm sorry, I lied."

"Yeah, whatever. I'm going to do you a solid." Jonathan shrugged his shoulders. "This Friday, you need to get off early and go home. Don't tell anyone what you're doing. Keep it to yourself."

"Why would I do that? What's the purpose?"

Simone got in her car. "All will be revealed if you do like I asked. Remember, I'm helping you."

Jonathan walked to her car window, "Did you send me those mysterious texts?"

She smiled, "I did. Do what I say."

She drove off, leaving Jonathan standing there. He got inside his car and thought about what Simone said. *"Why would she tell me to do this without telling me what it's about? Why go home early? Is this about Lea? Something must be happening, and she knows about it. I guess the only answer is to show up Friday and see what happens."*

Chapter 11

Jonathan sat in the townhouse waiting for Lea to come home from the club. She went out with her girls, but Jonathan believed that was a lie. He watched a couple of movies, but nothing took his mind off Lea. He called Terrance to see what he was up to, but he could not reach him either. That gnawing feeling of betrayal continued to reside in his spirit. The clock slowly made its way to two in the morning when the click at the door came. He watched her come in and instantly put the seductive, 'I love you' smile on her face. As each day rolled by, she reminded him more of himself.

"He, baby. I've been thinking about you all night. I just couldn't get away from those girls. Aaliyah especially. She's crazy."

Jonathan listened, but he continued not believe a word she said. Simone warned him about something Lea planned for the next day. He did not know how she planned to pull it off, but he was sure there would be a sign forthcoming. "That's cool baby. Why don't we hit the bed and get some in before we go to sleep?"

"Oh, sweetheart, I would love to take care of you, but I can't. I'm exhausted. I will make it up to you this weekend, I promise."

"Sure, I understand." Jonathan followed her into the bedroom. He got into bed and pretended everything was fine. Four hours later, Jonathan's alarm went off. He jumped up, thinking there was no way it could be six already. He looked over at Lea, who was fast asleep. She would sleep through a nuclear bomb. He tugged at her, "Hey, baby, it's time to get up." She mumbled something. Jonathan said again, "Lea, get up."

"I'm off today, babe. Remember, I worked that Saturday a few weeks back? They let me off today."

"Oh, you didn't tell me that." She rolled over and went back to sleep. Jonathan continued to get dressed, then he headed out to work. He did not tell her he got half the day off. Simone was sure whatever was to happen would happen around 12. He would likely get there at 12:30. Today, he would find out if Lea was the real deal or just a female version of himself.

He pulled up to work and went inside. His boss said, "Hey Jonathan, I know you're getting off early today, but can you do legal assistance for me?"

"Sure, Sergeant Miller."

"Thanks, you're awesome."

Jonathan smiled, "You're welcome." *"She may think I'm awesome, but it seems no one else does. My woman is cheating on me, and the prime suspect is my best friend. One best friend already turned on me and now I have this sinking feeling that I lost the best thing that I could ever have. If Lea is cheating, I know I can sweet talk Donna into getting back with me."*

Legal assistance was busy for a Friday morning, but Jonathan did not mind. It made the time roll by fast for him. When legal assistance was over, it was after nine. He had three more hours to go. Jonathan returned to his office in military justice to find Simone sitting there waiting for him. He said, "What are you doing here?"

"I just came by to see if you could get off today?"

"I said I would. Why don't you just tell me what all this is about?"

Simone sighed, "At first, I wanted to see you suffer, but I didn't want it to take forever, so I edged you in the right direction with the secret text. Now, I just want to see this end so, go home at 12. See what you see. Hell, I might be wrong." She uncrossed her legs and stood, "Vengeance is best served cold, but you don't have the heart for it… well, I don't have the heart for it. Go home and I hope I'm wrong."

Jonathan sighed, "That's a lot of code Simone when you could just tell me. Lea is cheating, isn't she?"

"You know we could have been great together, but you don't see me for the person I truly am. After watching you screw up with Donna, I can say the same thing about that relationship. You had it good twice, and you blew it." She shook her head and walked off.

Jonathan was furious now. She dared throw their relationship in his face, and his marriage to Donna. He would prove her and Donna wrong. He called his boy Terrance, "Hey Terrance, what's up? I tried to reach you last night."

"Man, I was with this, honey. I wasn't taking any calls last night. What did you need?"

"I just wanted to talk. Lea wasn't home. She said she was out with the girls. I don't know if I believe it."

"Man, why are you being so dedicated to her? Treat her like you did the others."

"Because, man, I truly love her."

Terrance replied, "What? Dude, you just got divorced and hooked up with Lea. how can you love her?"

"I don't know, but I do."

"Okay, man."

"I don't know what it is about her, but I know I love that woman. I can't get enough of her. This is the first time I have felt this way about a woman." The line

157

was silent. "Dude, I bared my soul, and you don't say anything."

"Man, what you're saying is scary. It doesn't sound like the boy I know. Even when you locked onto Donna, you never acted like that."

"Yeah, Donna was different. To be honest though, I've been thinking about her too. I screwed up with Donna. Donna would never betray me."

"Betrayed? You think Lea is tipping out on you? Man, she lives with you."

"I lived with Donna, and how did that turn out? It doesn't matter if you live with the person or not, you can find ways to cheat, and I think Lea's cheating. Hell, I cheated on Donna with her friend, so why would she be above that?"

"Dude, because she feels the same way about you that you feel about her."

"How do you know that?" An uncomfortable silence fell over the phone. Jonathan's suspicions grew. "Hey, man, I'm going to finish up some work and take my lunch at 11 today. I'll probably just grab a sandwich and eat on the beach. I need to sort some things out."

"Cool, bro. Let me know what you come up with?"

"Yeah, I will." Jonathan hung up the phone and leaned back in his chair. What he suspected had to be true. Terrance could not know Lea's feelings about him unless they talked. On one hand, he learned she truly loved him, but on the other, she had to be cheating on him with his best friend. He felt the sting of betrayal growing more and more. Simone must have gotten inside information on all of this for her to know the day and time Terrance and Lea would get together. Lea did not mention getting off until this morning. He reasoned she never told him because she wanted to be home alone so her lover could come over. He took a deep breath and let it out slowly. The noon hour could not come fast enough for him.

Jonathan starred at the clock. It was 15 minutes until the noon hour. Sergeant Rosa Pratt walked into his office. Sergeant Pratt was a reserve paralegal performing duty. She would take Jonathan's place the rest of the day. "Hey, Jonathan. You ready to get out of here?"

"I am, but I got a feeling it's not going to be be a good day."

"Aww, what you got planned?"

"Nothing." He cut his eyes at her. Jonathan had grown to trust Rosa. She only came in two days a month, but they became friends over the years. Female friends were something Jonathan did not have many of. "Look, I know I can trust you. I think my new girlfriend is cheating on me with my best friend. I'm going home to bust them."

"Oh, wow. That's not good at all. In your home? She should have more respect for you than that."

"Tell me about it. I mean, I can't say I don't deserve it. I had a good and loyal woman with Donna, and I blew it. Now, I'm reaping what I sowed. I can't believe Terrance would do this to me."

"I can't believe it either. You guys were so close."

"I know. We came into the Air Force at the same time. We went to basic and tech school together. I cross-trained but we never have lost a step with our friendship. I don't know why he would do this to me. Especially knowing I love this girl."

"Wow; love? You? That's something I haven't heard."

"Actually, with Lea, it's not really love… I'm realizing it's lust. Love is what I had with Donna, but I didn't want to admit it. She was attentive, loyal, dedicated, loving, caring… whatever positive you have in mind, that was Donna. I let lust destroy everything I had."

"Maybe it's not what you think it is. Sometimes we can blow things up in our head and believe them to be true. Just go home and see what's going on."

"Thanks, Rosa."

"Most of all, keep a level head."

Jonathan smiled. She knew how to keep him focused on the bigger picture. No matter how things turned out, he needed to keep a level head. His military career was more important than anything else at this point in his life. In addition, his basketball career was important. If he got into trouble, he would lose both.

The noon hour came, and Jonathan headed out the door. He imagined so many different scenarios when he got home, but tried with all his might to think of something else. He finally focused on the little girls who would never break his heart. No matter how the day turned for him, they would never let him down.

When he arrived, Lea's car was the only car in the driveway. He let out a deep sigh. *"Rosa was right. It was all in my head. I guess that's why Simone started backing out, saying she hoped she was wrong. You were wrong. You just wanted to get under my skin."* He parked his car and got out. When he got to the door, he found it opened. *"Hmm, Lea must have thought she closed it all the way."* He walked inside and there were rose pedals from the door up the stairs. He heard the sound that he hoped he would not hear. It was true, Lea was sleeping with someone else.

Jonathan took a deep breath. He remembered the words Rosa put into his spirit. Keeping calm at this moment would not be easy, but he had to keep his cool. For the sake of his girls, he could not lose his military career. Jonathan eased up the stairs to see who it was. He already suspected Terrance. When he got to the top of the stairs, he walked into the bedroom. Lea was on top of him making love to another man the way she made love to him. The pit in his stomach was unmatched by anything he felt in his life. Her flawless, naked body rode on top of him, and they both constantly bellowed out sounds of pleasure, the same sounds Jonathan made, the same feelings she made him feel when they were together.

Terrance's eyes opened. He quickly stopped. The emotions he bellowed out halted. Lea's confusion soon caused her to stop and look behind her. Neither of them could muster any words. Jonathan looked down. He didn't want to see anymore. The feeling of disgust enveloped him. He calmly said, "You have five minutes to get out of my house, both of you."

They each got up and got dressed. Terrance said, "Man…"

Jonathan held up his hand. "Don't say a word to me, punk, or we will be throwing down right now. Get out of my house."

Terrance rushed by him and down the stairs. Lea was next, but Jonathan grabbed her by the arm. He looked her in the eye, wondering why. "For the first time in my life, I loved someone, and that someone was you. Why did you do this to me?"

She let out a sighed, "I believe I'm built this way; guilt free sex, you know." She paused and sighed again, "I warned you on the ship. I asked you not to catch feelings. I am who I am. Someday, I may stop and settle down, but today isn't that day, Jonathan."

"Why my best friend?"

"Attraction; plus he didn't have feelings for me. Everything was great between you and me until you started talking marriage and moving in together. I loved the idea of moving in together and having a permanent boyfriend, but I wasn't ready to settle down. At first, Terrance turned me off, but somewhere, it clicked for me. Then he filled me in on the other women you were seeing along with me, Simone being one of them." Jonathan rolled his eyes. "Don't say it's not true because really it doesn't matter. Your feelings alone were enough to scare me away. Terrance, telling me about your other side pieces meant nothing. I actually respected that."

Jonathan nodded his head in disbelief. "I never cheated on you. I can't believe he told you that."

Lea continued, "Like I said, it didn't matter. What mattered most was that I could sleep with Terrance, and we went our separate ways." She looked him in his eyes. Her hazel eyes continued to captivate him, "Jonathan, I do love you, and I tried to be faithful, but in the end, I'm just like you. The difference with you is that Terrance wanted to tell you what was going, but I didn't. Terrance said I had to do it because you were best friends. When you caught me on the phone in the bathroom, I was talking to Terrance. You heard me yell at him because he needed to tell you. I didn't want you to find out this way. I'll be back to get my things."

Jonathan could not make eye contact with her. Her words cut deep into his soul. She gently patted him on the chest, pecked him on the cheek, and walked down the stairs. The sound of the door closing felt like a knife through his heart. He did not know if it was truly love or lust, but it felt painful. Lea's words sounded like the very words he uttered many times before; he could not control his lust.

Jonathan slid down the wall and dropped his head into his hands. He lost everything he had, chasing a woman who was just like him; she could not control her lust. He chased the excitement and got more than what he wanted. Now he found himself on his hallway floor doing something he had not done since his favorite uncle died. He cried.

Chapter 12

Jonathan did not know how long he sat on the floor or how many times the phone rang without him answering it. He did not care about anything. He wanted to curl up in a ball and die. Now he knew the pain he inflicted on so many others, especially his wife. Now he realized how many nights she must have felt the same way he did. It was unbearable and he could not understand how she put up with it for so long.

Jonathan found the strength to get off the floor. He walked into the bedroom and pulled the sheets off the bed. He wanted to burn them, but had no place to do it. Instead, he trashed everything and packed Lea's items. He wanted everything that was hers out of the house as soon as possible. His phone rang again. It was Simone. He knew she wanted to rub it in. "What do you want?"

"I'm actually sorry for you, Jonathan. I thought your boy would do the right thing, but like you, he couldn't. Why do you think the two of you got along so well?"

"I'm sure you're about to tell me."

"You're both the same. Both he and Ed wanted me, but you swooped in and took me. I don't know why I hooked up with you because you were dating my friend. I was just as stupid as Lea, but hey we all learned a lesson here today, didn't we?" Jonathan had nothing to say to her. "Nothing to say? Well, let me add a little more to the story for you. Last night Lea was with Ed. Terrance doesn't know about Ed, but I do. She was running the three of you, but you were the fool who caught feelings."

The line went dead. Simone had her revenge. She had the opportunity to sit back and watch Jonathan's life self-destruct. His only course of action now would be to see if he could revitalize the love Donna once had for him. He promised himself that if he could get her back, he would never cheat on her again. He would never lose her again. She provided the truest of love and she deserved to have it in return.

It was near six in the evening. Jonathan was dressed in his best casual outfit. He wanted to look good in his begging for Donna's hand back in marriage. He arrived at the duplex, where he once called home. Donna's car sat in the driveway. There was another car there that he did not recognize. He suspected it was one of her girls. They always hung out together. *"Got my roses, got some treats for my little darlings and a bottle of wine for later this evening. Donna, baby, I don't know what I need to do to win you back, but I'm prepared for it."*

Jonathan tapped on the door, and it opened as if she were expecting him. The girls shouted 'daddy' and gave him a hug. He gave them their treats and smiled. They were happy to see him and happier to get the treats. He looked at Donna. "Can I talk to you for a minute outside?" Donna nodded her acceptance, and they walked outside. "So, I've done a lot of soul searching the last few hours and I really screwed up Donna. I mean, you and the kids… I really messed up."

"Yes, you did, and I guess you found out about your friends. They were never your friends. Since this came out, both your boys tried to get with me. You might know that Ed told me about your escapades, but Terrance hit on me from the beginning. He never told me what you were doing. I guess that was beneath him, but he certainly tried to sleep with me. When you were in Saudi, he called almost every day, two and three times a day, begging me to go out with him."

"Why didn't you tell me?"

"Because you wouldn't have believed me, Jonathan. We both know that."

Jonathan looked down, "You're probably right. I've been on a destructive course for a while now, but I'm better. I just need another chance to make it right.

I'm even giving up basketball because that's what led to my lust."

"I'm sorry, Jonathan, but what we had is over."

"It's never over, Donna. I brought you these and some wine. Let's enjoy the evening. No sex, just enjoy each other's company." Donna refused to take the items. Instead, she opened the door and motioned for someone to join them. Jonathan looked at him with disgust. "What are you doing with my wife?"

Donna said, "With all due respect, Jonathan, I'm not your wife anymore. Mike Hollinger is a good man, and we are dating. Guess what? Until we are married, I don't need to have sex with him. I should have been with a Christian man from the beginning, but I allowed you into my life. I fell in love with the basketball superstar that every other woman on base loved. You didn't just destroy yourself, you destroyed me, the kids, and who knows how many women who worshipped your basketball skills. But now, I'm back in the church and re-making my life. I'm not going back to you." She turned to walk back into the house. "Jonathan, you are not healed. Find someone to talk to so you can rid yourself of that lustful spirit. I'll see you next week when you come get the girls."

She walked back inside and for the second time in one day, the sound of a door closing felt like a knife through his heart. Jonathan returned to his vehicle and then to his house. He found himself stuck in a lease that he could not pay and alone for the first time in his adult life, with no companionship.

The next morning Jonathan wrote in his new journal, *"Rat-a-tat-tat… the rain pounded my windows as I laid awake in my bed alone. The woman I thought I loved would no longer be with me, and the woman I should have loved did not desire me anymore. I stared at the ceiling, wondering how I allowed my life to go wrong. What did I do to draw God's ire against me? The conclusion was simple, yet complex. I didn't draw His ire; I had His love, but the enemy wanted me to believe I wasn't a child of the most high. I let the enemy use my peers in the streets to teach me the myths about woman. They are only notches for my bedpost; to be a man, I had to sleep with as many as possible and that every man cheats. Most men do cheat until they meet their match; a woman he thinks he loves who cheats on him."*

"Prince once said, 'Love and lust, they both have four letters, but they are entirely different words.' He was so correct. Donna was the definition of love; I was the definition of lust."

"I listened to the sound of the rain, worried that my life as I knew it was over, but something, maybe what my grandmother used to teach me, pulled at my heart. Maybe it was the Spirit of the Lord telling me to hang in there. She often told me that God talks to us all the time, but we can't hear him because we are so engulfed in sin. When we stop sinning, we hear Him clearer. That voice seems to tell me it's time to stop. It's time to go home to the church and do as Donna did, clean up my life. Get things right. God is funny sometimes. He used the very lust I had to bring me to my knees and into His bosom. I know my life

is not over. In fact, it's just beginning. The rat-a-tat-tat of the rain continued to fall as I drift back to sleep. However, this time I am at peace knowing that the days ahead will be filled with my work for the Lord."

GERALD C. ANDERSON, SR.

Why I Wrote

This Book

Let me get this question out of the way first, no it's not about me. I know when people read my books; they think it's about me or how I feel. Not so most of the time. This is certainly not about me in its entirety, but it comprises pieces of stories I have witnessed in my life. Some of which are mine.

In Love & Lust, I wanted to capture the cheating side of a young man. He's admired by many of the young ladies on his base because of his ability to play a sport, in this case, basketball. What he doesn't realize is his friends hate him because of this admiration.

Jonathan falls in love with Donna Williams and later marries her. However, he doesn't appreciate what he has in Donna and is always looking for something on the side.

Jonathan says he's like this because he was trained to be the way he is. He didn't have a father figure at home, so he learned how to treat women from the streets. This is not the way to go.

My experience in my young life was much the same. We didn't respect women; they were a challenge. Boys are teased if they haven't had sex by a certain age. Those who had multiple women were admired and respected, but those who held themselves out for the one were teased.

In my early twenties, I used to boast about how many women I was running at the same time. In hindsight, I was a fool. At least one of those women should have been my wife and it would have lasted forever, had I appreciated who she was. Like Jonathan, I learned my lesson when God brought me to my knees at the hands of a woman. At that point, I gave my life to Christ and tried to do better.

It wasn't until I was in my forties that I truly learned to respect women. Infidelity was something that should never be practiced. A pastor once told me that giving your heart to someone is dangerous. Jonathan gave his heart to Lea, and she abused it. If Jonathan took the pastor's advance and gave his heart to Jesus, he would have been much better off.

GERALD C. ANDERSON, SR.

I hope this novella touches the hearts and mind of those who choose lust for the opposite sex. Find the right person and settle down with him/her. Remember, the grass is not greener on the other side.

Author Bio

Gerald C. Anderson, Sr. was born and raised in Tampa, Florida. He spent most of his childhood life growing up in the Belmont Heights area of Tampa.

In 1980, Gerald graduated from C. Leon King Senior High School in Temple Terrace, Florida. Following graduation, he enlisted in the United States Air Force.

Air Force Life

In his service career, Gerald traveled the world with assignments to California (twice), Florida, Kansas, Maryland, West Germany, and Korea. Upon his last assignment in Maryland and after retirement from the Air Force, Gerald began working in the United States Federal Government's Department of Energy. In 2003, he moved to the Internal Revenue Service, and in 2007 he joined the Department of Education.

GERALD C. ANDERSON, SR.

Education

In 2005, Gerald got his Bachelor of Science degree in Computer Information Systems from Strayer University, and in 2008 he received his Master of Administration degree in Criminal Justice Administration from the University of Cincinnati (UC).

Published Books

We Come in Peace

27 Hours (What Would You Do If You Faced the End?)

Standing Firm (One Family's Fight Against Domestic Violence)

Secrets (Silent Screams in The Dark)

The Last Song

The Lawyer

Saved

The Room

Are You Innocent?

The Compendium Series

Weight Loss

Warlord

The Last Honorable Man

The Dream

The Death Knights

Twins

The Ride Along

Creative Inspirations

Fatal Misperceptions

A Saved Man

In 1992, Gerald turned his life over to Jesus Christ and a life with Christ at the head. He is a musician in church. He continues to live in Maryland with his son.

Thank You!

I would like to take this opportunity to thank you for reading my novella. "Love & Lust" was written to entertain my fanbase. I hope I carried out this goal, and you have enjoyed the story and maybe learned something from it.

Please consider reading my earlier novels, novellas and short stories listed at the front of this novel. I also manage a Christian lifestyle magazine, "The Lyfe Magazine" (www.thelyfemagazine.com).

Last, if you enjoyed this novella, please go to Amazon and write me a review. Reviews help move novels, novellas and short stories on Amazon so that other potential readers can find it.

Thank you so much and always have a blessed day!

Gerald C. Anderson, Sr.

Made in the USA
Las Vegas, NV
21 February 2023